Witch in the Lighthouse

Azalea Forrest

ISBN: 1983581445

ISBN-13: 978-1983581441

Cover design by Math Graphics & Audio.

Mathematician Records
Florida

www.azaleaforrest.wordpress.com
www.mathematicianrecords.com

ACKNOWLEDGMENTS

I'd like to thank the artists and animators that have inspired me throughout my life. There are too many to name. My friends, for their encouragement and help in editing. And my partner, for always being there for me.

CONTENTS

PROLOGUE

Sunlight shone down through the roof of the greenhouse, warming the redhead's freckled cheeks while the smell of fresh earth and flowers filled the air. The floor, a mixture of dirt and cobblestone, felt warm and inviting beneath her bare feet. Magnolia Hanna smiled to herself as she clipped chamomile flowers from a shelf of plants with her grandmother Sophie who, although shriveled by the years, was still a charming presence to her granddaughter.

"We'll dry these for the old Parker couple and I'll show you how to give it a good spark, dear." Grandma Sophie laughed with vigor despite her age. She elbowed her granddaughter in jest and Maggie elbowed her in return as they both chuckled at the idea of giving a love potion to their neighbors.

"Grandmother!" Maggie laughed and attempted a stern expression at her elder. Sophie gave her a sly look. The young woman collected lavender, basil and mint, each feeling resinous against her fingers and a smidge sticky, then clipped a sunflower from its stalk and placed them all on a drying rack nearby with the chamomile. All but the flowers gave off a strong scent, but each played well against the other, like tea on a warm summer's day.

"I thought we weren't supposed to judge a customer in need?" she continued.

"My dear, give an old woman a break. These bones are due for a good teasing if they're to make an aphrodisiac for the *Parkers*."

"It did take them a bit of courage to approach us," Maggie commented, but still, she smiled.

"Perhaps they'll appreciate our services a bit more, then. You'd think they would have moved out of town by now if they were really so bothered. Batty old fools."

Magnolia rolled her eyes as she adjusted a hefty potted plant so the leaves would stretch out more evenly. The look was of endearment: Grandma Sophie was as energetic as ever.

The Parkers weren't all that bad. They were new to the lives of witches and had moved to the town of Emelle to be closer to their family, who happened to be witches themselves. In fact, most of the villagers were witches. Not all of them had the potion prowess that Grandma Sophie had, however, which was why Sophie and her granddaughter dried the herbs for the Parker's potion now.

No, witches had all sorts of specialties and professions in Emelle. Some enchanted clothing, some were farmers, some were even carpenters and potters. There was a librarian witch, a fire-fighting witch and even a mechanic witch. Emelle had a quaint population, but everyone tried to be useful in their own way. Some *did* dabble in potion making, but Grandma Sophie was the expert.

Magnolia stood from beside the pot on the floor and wiped her hands on her apron, which was tan in color with little plants and flowers detailed in the top corners. It covered the yellow dress she wore beneath. Her mother had made the apron and Maggie couldn't get over how cute it was.

"Well, we're done for now, aren't we?" Maggie began untying her apron, ready to end the day.

Sophie sighed. "Youth," she said, smiling. "Ever eager.

2

Yes dear, for now. Let's take a break in the house, shall we?"

Maggie hung her apron on the hook by the door and picked up the hat that sat on its rack beside it. While she didn't regularly wear the customary black garb—and no one in her village seemed to do so anymore, either—she at least wore the pointed black hat. She grinned at her grandmother and received a small bow in return.

Grandma Sophie used her cane to hobble across the greenhouse to where Maggie held the door. Once she was through, Maggie followed, and they walked back to the family home together.

Stepping stones were laid casually in the earth and they led to the two story white house of the Hanna's. Runes were carved into some of the stones and steps that led up the wrap-around porch, where plants and small statues decorated the floorboards and windows. Maggie helped her grandmother up the few steps and opened the screen door. There, the redhead stopped to see her mother sitting in the kitchen, holding a letter and crying.

"Mom?" Maggie hurried into the kitchen and put her hand on the table, close to her mother's hand. Sophie stood in the doorway and adjusted her glasses as she took in her daughter's condition.

"What's wrong, dear?" Grandma Sophie asked.

"It's Tom," Amora wept. "He's died of a heart attack." Leaning back in her chair, she lowered the letter to the table and covered her eyes with one hand.

Magnolia and Sophie both blanched, but it was Grandma Sophie that walked into the kitchen and put her hand upon her daughter's back. Maggie was too stunned to do much of anything but stand there, staring at the letter shaking in her mother's grip.

Tom was Amora's brother-in-law, but they were all very close. For him to die so suddenly and so young was shocking.

"Amora, where's Daniel?" Grandma Sophie asked, the sadness apparent in her own voice.

Magnolia's mother shook her head, unable to answer, and Sophie looked to Maggie.

"Fetch your father, dear. Go on."

Maggie dashed from the room, one hand already struggling to brush the tears from her eyes.

~*~

The next few weeks had been filled with meetings and letters, discussing the funeral and going over the will. At the end of it all, Maggie was sitting in her room wrapped in blankets and staring at a paper. It was a personal letter from Uncle Thomas that was included with his will.

"Dear Magpie,

I can imagine this letter doesn't find you well. I am sorry for that, but it seems I have passed. Excuse me if this comes off as rather queer. You see, I've had a share of strange feelings lately. I felt it imperative to write this out and let you know how much I love and miss you and the family.

I'm sure Daniel is happy in his hovel, and I say that lovingly. So in the event of my passing, I want you to have the lighthouse. Please, take care of it, if you would have it. I know you loved it as a child, and in our letters you seem to still comment on it affectionately. I think the town would be happy to have a competent witch taking care of the lighthouse; I think you'd do a better job than an old man like me and with time to spare. Once they get to know you, they'll warm up.

I love you, Magnolia. And the family, too.

~Thomas"

Tom had always written a bit differently than how he spoke in person and it always made her laugh, even during a serious matter such as this and even through the tears. It was always prim and proper.

She wiped her eyes and sat the letter down in her lap. When she was little, Tom would hold her hand as they climbed the lighthouse stairwell together. Every time she reached the top, she would be amazed at how far she could see. She felt like a giant, and Tom would tell her so. She remembered when they would drink hot chocolate in his living room, especially when it rained... The tears had come again, and she hadn't even noticed. *I should have gone to see him again,* she thought bitterly. But she couldn't let the grief take over, so she drew a deep, shaky breath.

Maggie had never dreamed she would own the lighthouse, nor that her uncle would pass so soon. It was so sudden, and she was anxious to think of moving away from home. She had been thinking of going to visit her uncle before all this happened, that was true. She might have even considered living with him, if he would have had her.

Being close to her family, it was difficult to part from them, and now that Tom was gone, being alone in that empty lighthouse full of memories almost made her feel paralyzed. But, she was a proper witch now and considered an adult at twenty-one, so maybe it was the right time. This was a real opportunity to grow and be independent, despite the unhappy circumstance. She did miss the town, and the smell of the ocean...and especially the lighthouse up on the hill. What she missed most, though, she would never see again.

Still, she managed to smile. Tom wanted her to have it, so she would accept it. Someone needed to take care of the old spire, after all, and she did have fond memories of it. When she really got down to her feelings, and she always tried to be honest with herself, she would love to own the lighthouse. This would be a new beginning. She could share her magic and make new friends.

A tear, and then another, ran down her face. She lifted a hand, quietly laughing, to wipe them away. Gods, she missed him.

The idea of spending another moment moping in her room was suddenly abhorrent. She gently folded the letter and placed it on her nightstand. With a flourish, she threw the blankets still covering her to the floor and stood. Placing her hands on her hips, she surveyed her belongings, her eyes still red and puffy, but her heart full of hope.

It was time to pack.

~*~

Magnolia stayed for the funeral but as soon as it was over, she had her pack prepared and was ready to leave the next morning. She viewed her uncle's grave once more, where it stood at the forest's edge in Emelle's cemetery. Ferns crept out from the forest, peeking out along the edge of the treeline, and a lone dogwood grew outside of the pine to offer shade over Tom's grave. The leaves of the dogwood were as white as snow, and had been grown from magic. Maggie left more flowers on his tombstone and a drawing of his lighthouse, as if solidifying her promise and her farewell.

On the family porch, she hugged her parents goodbye.

"Are you sure you need to leave today?" Her father brushed some of Maggie's hair from her face. He was tall like his late brother, but willowy in comparison to Tom's stocky demeanor. Amora held onto his arm, forlorn but smiling through it all.

"Yes," Maggie said, positive. "If I stay any longer, I might not leave at all." She forced a smile to match her mother's.

"Be careful. You can visit us any time. We'd love to visit you when you're settled." Amora hugged her daughter again, then so did Daniel and Grandma Sophie.

"I'll write to you soon, don't worry. I love you! Say goodbye again for me to everyone." She hadn't wanted them to be there on her final goodbye, just in case she needed another cry. It wasn't that she was ashamed of her emotions, not really, but it was hard enough as it was.

Maggie made her way down the steps and into the garden. The grass made a soft crunch beneath her boots and she wondered when she would walk back up her family's porch again. With her broom in hand, she sat upon it and almost lazily lifted up into the air, the rucksack on her back not bothering her flight in the slightest.

She waved her final goodbye, seeing tears in her father's eyes. She couldn't blame him, even as she hid her own. Her mother cried freely, but Grandma Sophie was cheering Maggie on with that big, mischievous grin on her face. Magnolia flew up higher into the sky and away from home towards the sea. Her pack was full of memories and gifts to see her on her new journey.

The breeze felt rejuvenating even as she watched her little town disappear into the forest. It washed away her current apprehensions and worries and replaced them with hope and an idea of, perhaps, filling in her uncle's shoes. It might just be a lighthouse, but it had been his life. It was a time for Maggie to be independent and really rely on her witchiness.

She might not have her uncle's carpentry skills, or his knowledge of lights or machinery, but she could repair things, and clean and do other maintenance with her magic. Of course, learning new skills never hurt anyone, either. She was sure the town could use some potions, too, and with her training from her grandmother, she knew she could brew up something strong for whatever their needs.

Her travels were uneventful, though pleasant, and she arrived in Lightview at dusk. She flew over the town at a distance and made her way up the hill to where her lighthouse sat, its light shining on across the cliff. The lighthouse was attached to a home made of red brick and stone. Faded navy blue spiraled up the white exterior, but other than faded paint it didn't look as if it was in disrepair. Despite her current feelings of grief, she found herself smiling. It still looked like home, just as she remembered it.

Maggie flicked on the lights, lit the hearth with her wand and sat her bag down on the floor. Everything still looked the same. Nothing had been moved, nothing that she could remember. She wondered if her uncle would have rather been buried here than back home, but his will had specified that after spending his living life away from his family, the least he could do was rest his bones in Emelle. In a way, she might have felt less lonely if she could visit him here. But no, this had been for the best.

She touched the mantle affectionately as she looked over the items sitting upon it. Her gaze fell on a picture of the family smiling happily at the camera and she felt a touch of emotion sting her eyes. It would have been nice to have one last gathering together.

"Oh, er. Hullo there!"

Startled, Maggie turned to see someone standing in the archway that led to the lighthouse stairwell. It was a man standing there, and he laughed and sheepishly rubbed the back of his head.

"Didn't mean to scare ya'. Honestly, you surprised *me*! Are you the new owner?" He was a tall man, and round, but he looked strong. He had kind eyes.

Maggie gripped her broom self-consciously and nodded. "Yes," she managed. And then she stood a little straighter, smiling again. "I'm Magnolia."

The man eyed the broom with some curiosity but he grinned and reached his hand out to her for a shake. "I'm Mikel. I own a produce stand down in the market, but it was my turn to check on the light today. There's a few of us that have been takin' shifts from town. It's a pleasure to meet you." They shook hands. "Why don't I make you some tea, help you settle in? Got any belongings that need to be moved proper?"

Maggie shook her head no and gestured to her rucksack on the floor. "I only brought what I could carry. Luckily for me, everything else I'd need is already here. I wouldn't mind some tea, though."

Mikel clapped his hands together. "Excellent. I could fancy myself a cup as well." Rubbing his hands together excitedly, he headed off towards the kitchen.

Maggie followed and found herself in the same familiar, comfortable kitchen with a round wooden table sitting beside the window. She sat there while Mikel turned the kettle on. It was a homey, rustic kitchen with an electric stove that looked like it might also burn wood, and there was a refrigerator, too. A small window sat above the sink and a second larger one looked out at the bluff from the kitchen table in the corner. She remembered that Uncle Tom had liked to cook, so there were plenty of spices and cooking utensils.

"It's a shame what happened to Tom," Mikel said sadly. He was setting up the cups and sugar. "Did you know him?"

Maggie gave a half smile as she looked at Mikel. "He was my uncle."

"Oh!" Mikel averted his gaze as if he should have known already, and then slowly looked back at her. "I'm sorry, lass. He was a real help around town, y'know. Everyone loved him." He looked Maggie over for a short moment before taking the kettle off the stove. He poured the tea. "I thought you looked a bit young. You're not here on your own, are you?"

"I am. But it's fine. I'm happy to take over for my uncle. I stayed here for a bit when I was little, so I have fond memories of this place, even still." She leaned forward in her seat slightly. "Just honey, please."

Mikel brought Maggie her cup and sat with her at the table. "It's a hard job maintaining the lighthouse. But Tom lived for it. He had a love for these hills, the sea, and the sights at the top of the light. He used to say it was the closest he got to flying." He eyed the broom Maggie had sat in the corner of the room. "I don't think you'll have as much trouble, though, being a witch and all."

"You can tell?" Even with her hat and broom, most outsiders didn't recognize a witch when they saw one.

"Aye. There hasn't been a witch here in a long time, but I'm not unfamiliar." He gave her a knowing look, almost sad.

"I wouldn't worry too much, but there's a few here that don't shine too kindly on witch-folk. Don't take it personally."

"Oh." Maggie remembered her uncle's letter. "I'm sure they'll warm up to me."

Mikel laughed and slapped his knee. "That's the spirit! Now, if ya' need anything, you just give me a holler. I live off of Naia Street, just around the corner from the market. It's a bit late to be showin' you around, but you oughter go down there n' have a look as soon as you feel up to it. It's about time I got back to the wife." He downed his tea, set his cup in the sink and then squeezed Maggie's shoulder affectionately.

"Thanks for the tea. It was wonderful to meet you, Mikel." She squeezed his hand in return, honestly grateful.

"And you, lass! Someone'll be by to show you the ropes of how this old light works. I'll let 'em know in the mornin'. Here's the key, n'you have a good night now."

The screen door lightly knocked shut and Magnolia sat alone in the kitchen, nursing her tea and holding the key to her uncle's lighthouse tightly in one hand. She stared down into the swirling mug and felt a mixture of emotions. The hot liquid made her feel a bit more normal, at least.

She made her way back into the living room with her broom and set it beside the door, and then hung the key from its ring on the rack. She picked up her rucksack only to set it down on the couch in front of the fire. All she wanted now was to sleep, but she couldn't even imagine going up to her uncle's room and using his bed, not yet. So she laid down on the couch and hugged her bag instead. Her long trip had been exhausting and she couldn't deny that she felt a little overwhelmed.

Sleep came easy; it wrapped her like a blanket. And thankfully, it was dreamless.

CHAPTER ONE

There was something about the sea breeze that was comforting to Magnolia. It was the smell. It was always with her, and when it wasn't, it was suddenly all the more powerful when it was again. If she could, she would wrap her arms around it. She would kiss it. That was how much she felt the sea breeze comforted her.

But Maggie was unable to feel comforted by the breeze now.

She stood in a shop where the breeze couldn't reach her. She held new threads and needles in her hands, clutched to her chest, as she anxiously waited for her turn in line.

It was a lovely little shop with dozens upon dozens of tiny boxes lined up on tables and shelves, filled with different items of almost anything one could possibly need. There were books, too, and twine, aprons and work gloves... But the other customers looked at her uncomfortably or didn't look at her at all.

It wasn't that she was particularly odd looking. In fact, she looked rather nice. She was of average height, with long, fall colored hair wrapped in a braid. She wore an oversized sweater that fit like a loose dress, black stockings and brown boots. Freckles sat, sun-kissed, on her nose and cheeks.

Perhaps it was that she was fidgeting. She bobbed one knee forward and back and her fingers flicked the fabric wrapped around the new needles. She didn't make eye contact with anyone, as she felt a bit anxious herself.

No, it wasn't that she was fidgeting.

It was Maggie's turn. She stepped up to pay and gently placed her items on the counter. The clerk, an old woman with short, gray hair, looked at Maggie over her half-moon glasses with contempt.

"We don't serve witches in this shop." Her tone matched her glare; severe and biting.

Magnolia stared at the clerk as if she had misheard. That couldn't be true, she had been served here before. Not by this woman, but...

"Ma'am, are you sure?" Magnolia pulled out the allotted amount of copper coins. "I have enough money..."

"We don't serve witches and your money's no good here." The clerk knocked the counter with what sounded like her knee, or perhaps a cane. It made Magnolia jump. She looked around herself, trying not to appear too upset and checking the looks around her. No one seemed to pay her any mind and seemed to intentionally avert their eyes.

Maggie lowered her head and stepped away from the counter. She had been able to purchase items there just last week, why was now suddenly different? Just because she was a witch? She knew she wasn't exactly well received by all the townsfolk in Lightview, but she just wanted new needles and thread... Mikel's warning hadn't made this any easier. to swallow.

Dejected, Magnolia left the shop, leaving her items behind on the counter.

The street was the stark opposite of how she currently felt: sunny, positive and full of life. Pedestrians chatted together jovially and a dog played with a child in front of the flower shop.

She caught a few glances, some with hard expressions,

and Maggie tried hard to manage a smile in spite of them. She stood a few feet outside of the general store with her hands clasped together in front of her, holding her money purse tight. This hadn't been her only reason for coming into town today, but it had been what she was most excited about. She had clothes to mend and curtains to sew. She had broken her last needle and there were some things she just didn't want to do with magic alone.

"I am so sorry."

Magnolia spun around, pulling her purse up to her chest in surprise.

"My grandmother, she's prejudiced against *anyone* different..." The young man thrust his hands towards Magnolia and she clumsily accepted what he handed her, almost dropping her purse in the process. "Please accept this as an apology." He lowered his head so low it was almost a bow and he rubbed the back of it with embarrassment.

Magnolia stared at the items the young man had given her. It was the thread and needles she had tried to purchase.

"You don't have to do this," Maggie said quickly. "I'd rather not get you in trouble when I could find this somewhere else." It was obvious it wasn't just anyone different, but specifically witches that his grandmother didn't like. Maybe he was just trying to make her feel better.

The young man stood straight again and pushed his glasses up the bridge of his nose. "Please. It's the least I can do. We would love to keep your business and I won't allow that kind of behavior in my shop." His hands were laced together in a plea.

Magnolia found herself smiling, albeit sheepishly. *His* shop? He was a bit young, no older than her, anyway. She lifted the items he had given her and canted her head a little, feeling shy. "Thank you. I really appreciate that." She tucked the items and her money purse into the satchel around her shoulder. "But aren't you supposed to heed your elders?"

The young man chuckled. "If we listened to everything

Old Nan said, we'd be out of business. I'm Canton Val. You live in the lighthouse, right?" He extended his hand to hers, which she shook.

"Yes." She smiled. "I'm Maggie."

"It's nice to finally meet you. I've seen you in the shop before. Don't be afraid to come back, okay? I'll make sure Nan doesn't try and run you off again. As far as I'm concerned, you deserve to shop just like anyone else. Witch or not."

Maggie felt a little shocked by his declaration. Besides Mikel, Canton had been the first to openly accept her. "Thank you," she said, smiling so hard she felt her cheeks go pink. "I'll come by again, definitely."

They waved their goodbyes and Maggie started off down the cobblestone street towards the market. Her spirits soared and she held onto her satchel with one hand fondly.

The market was thriving. It was full of local vendors that either couldn't afford a storefront or those who didn't need one. There were several competing farmer stands, but Maggie's favorite was Mikel's. He always had the freshest vegetables and he was always jovial. Best of all, it was family run, and they were all just as good spirited as Mikel. Lately, though, it was just him and his wife working. She didn't mind either way.

For the most part, people either avoided Maggie altogether or they were just kind enough to pass as polite. Word of her witchiness had spread fast, but she had been living in Lightview for a little while now and while the people weren't always helping her feel welcome, she still loved the town and the lighthouse. She made her way through the crowds until she reached Mikel's stand.

"You're lookin' pretty chipper today, lass," Mikel noted.

Maggie's grip on her bag tightened slightly.

"Any townsfolk givin' you a hard time about your witchiness?" He gestured at her and saw her agreeable expression.

"Somewhat," she admitted.

"Don't be worryin' none. We all loved your uncle. Some just don't bode well with change. And let's be honest... You're quite the breath of fresh air." He winked at her.

Maggie laughed. "Thanks, Mikel... Uncle Thomas wasn't so ordinary, though. He didn't use magic, but he wasn't exactly traditional."

"Aye." Mikel bellowed a laugh. "That's what was so great about him! But he was a part of this town. The heart of the lighthouse! He was dependable and easy going, and more willing than most to accept outsiders." He gave her a knowing smile. "A lot of these folks, they don't remember you as a child... Witches haven't been around these parts in some time. But they'll warm up to ya', eventually."

"Yeah..." Maggie smiled. She loved hearing about her uncle and remembering her childhood with him. It hadn't been that long, but as a child, the memories felt like they could have lasted years. "I wasn't exactly a known witch then anyway, was I?" She winked as if it had been a secret, and then she laughed. Mikel was a nice man. He was a little round and a bit older, but he must have been around the same age as her parents. He reminded her of Tom and her father.

"Nah, you weren't. But you'll see. Listen—" He leaned forward. "The Harvest Festival is comin' up soon. Everyone gets together and we have a good old time. People'll be used to ya' by then. N'if not, who needs 'em, eh?"

"Right! Who needs 'em!" said Prairie, Mikel's wife. She was brandishing carrots like a weapon from around the stand. She had a big grin on her face and tomato juice spilled on her apron, as if from battle. She gave a fierce expression and it made Maggie laugh.

"Right!" Maggie nodded and covered her mouth as she giggled. "Thank you both, as always."

~*~

The way back to Magnolia's home was a lovely walk. From cobblestone streets and decorated storefronts, the stores turned into homes. Gardens reached out into tall grass that led all the way up the peninsula to where Maggie lived. She had the option to cross a small bridge, as the connection between her island and the mainland would fill during particularly high tides, but it was dry now, so she simply walked across the canal and then continued up the hill. She liked to look at the small stones and bugs that lived there in the canal, so she welcomed the chance to walk through it.

Boulders lined one side of the lighthouse for protection from storms but the land was fertile and unabused. Wildflowers grew everywhere and a few trees grew where they could. The lighthouse was a faded white and navy, with paint chipped from the sun and sea breeze. The light still spun dutifully, ever on for any unpredictable weather event.

Maggie made her way up the stone steps and noted the cans of paint by her front door. Someone must have dropped them off while she was away. She thought that was rather kind of them; even with magic it would have been a bother to carry them all the way from town to home. Then again, she wondered if someone was simply saying, *Get to work!*

She tried not to think about it.

Maggie held open the screen door with her hip as she unlocked the front door and stepped inside, her bags hanging from her arms. The outside of the home was layered in red bricks, but the inside was all beautiful, natural stone and wood. Herbs dried from the ceiling and a faint smell of lavender and sage filled the room. She set the bags down on a small table and pulled her wand from her satchel. Pointing it at the fireplace, she made a small movement with it, as if she was painting on an invisible surface, and the hearth came to life with a small flame. Another flicking movement and all the windows in the room opened. A mixture of heat with the sea breeze lulled her into a safe sense of calm.

As she put her food away in the kitchen, there was a

knock at her door. She poked her head out from the kitchen archway and saw someone she didn't recognize through the door's window.

"Hello?" The girl looked around from behind the door. Maggie imagined she couldn't see much until the witch stepped out into the light of the living room to answer. The stranger was a young woman with light brown hair tied up in a messy, braided bun. Her face lit up when she saw Maggie come to the door. "Oh, you must be Magnolia!"

Maggie opened the front door and stepped out onto the porch, her hand holding onto the screen door. "Yes, I am. Who...?"

"I'm Bea!" Bea picked up one of the paint cans next to the door and her smile seemed to widen. "Canton asked me to bring you some paint after he spoke with you this morning. I knocked earlier, but you weren't here, so I was looking around the grounds when I heard you coming up the steps. I hope that's alright?" She smiled sheepishly. "They're on the house. After all, the lighthouse is important to all of us."

Maggie's mouth opened in surprise before she found herself chuckling behind her hand in relief. She wasn't being rushed to clean up after all. In fact, she was making very nice friends.

"Hello, Bea. It's nice to meet you. You know Canton?"

"Of course! He's my brother. He remembered hearing that the lighthouse needed a fresh coat of paint. Since he asked me to bring them by, I thought I could help you out! Will you be painting any time soon?"

Maggie looked back into her house to think for a moment. She did have a few things to do...but this girl had brought these cans all the way here, and... "How did you carry all these?"

"Do you think I flew them over?" Bea winked.

Maggie cupped her chin in one hand and supported her elbow with her other arm, smiling doubtfully.

Bea laughed. "We have a cart, silly. I parked it around the

17

house." She pointed towards the end of the porch. Maggie could just barely see it poking out from around the corner. She was surprised she hadn't seen it earlier; its exposed engine was enormous and glared in the sunlight.

Maggie sighed, but she smiled. "I guess we could get some painting done. You did me a real favor. Thank you."

Bea clapped her hands together and grabbed another paint can. "Great! So..." She looked up to the top of the lighthouse. "How, um... Will we climb?"

Maggie lifted an index finger, so as to hold her a moment, and ran inside only to run back out again holding her broom. She found herself grinning, but she did feel a bit nervous. What if flying was too much for Bea? She knew Magnolia was a witch already...

"Flying?!"

"O-of course." She lowered her broom slightly, unsure.

"That's amazing!" Bea would have thrown the paint cans into the air if they weren't so heavy, but she lifted them some with glee. "Let's see, then!"

Maggie rubbed the back of her head, embarrassed. She hadn't seen such enthusiasm for her witchery since she left home. It was refreshing and...well, it made her feel normal.

"Okay," she said, chuckling.

She stepped down into the grass and turned around to face Bea. It had been some time since she'd last flown. Knowing the villagers didn't take too kindly to magic, she didn't want to upset them any more by flagrantly throwing it in their faces. Walking had sufficed for the time being.

Taking a deep breath, she placed her broom beside her and sat on it, side saddle. It held her obediently and slowly lifted her several feet off the ground. Wind seemed to rush around her, fluttering her hair and clothes.

Bea ran down the steps with her mouth open in surprise and dropped the cans at her feet. "I can hardly believe it... I've never seen a person fly!" She laughed out loud as Maggie flew higher towards the top of the lighthouse.

Maggie circled around the towering spire with elation. It felt so wonderful to be up in the air again like this. Back in Emelle, she would fly every day, but being in Lightview, she didn't want to make anyone uncomfortable by showing off her witchiness more than she had to. It was already difficult enough just walking through the streets and trying to make acquaintances. Sometimes, people just didn't understand magic and were bound to take it the wrong way. She had heard enough stories to know that. Experiencing it was just a lot different than she imagined.

It was cool and breezy, being up there around the top of the lighthouse, but she felt in control. Maggie circled around a second time and listened as the seagulls cried in the distance. The ocean spread out before her, seemingly endless against the blue sky and fluffy white clouds. She circled one final time before coming back down to float beside Beatrice.

"That was amazing! I've heard of humans flying, and let's be honest—I thought it was balderdash. But to actually *see* it... That's something else entirely!" Beatrice looked like she was about to bounce right out of her shoes, she was so excited. Maggie just laughed.

"I hear there hasn't been a witch in town for quite some time." Maggie smiled then, and not unkindly.

"It's true." Bea gave a sheepish grin as she started to relax and put one hand on her hip. "I thought Canton was pulling my leg when he told me a witch moved into town."

"Do you work at the store? I've never seen you there."

"Yeah, sometimes. I haven't been working as much since I started schooling."

"Oh, what are you going for?"

"I'm learning about marine wildlife. Being a port and fishing town can be hard on the wildlife and the fisheries. I'd like to think I could help."

"That's promising. I don't know much about the ocean, myself. My hometown is in the mountains." Maggie used her wand to summon some items from inside her home. Paint brushes and rollers floated across Bea's vision and Maggie's magic placed them on the grass by their feet. Bea gave an excited gasp and Maggie found herself smiling still, her cheeks going red.

"Well, let's get started."

Bea happily took moments out of her painting the base of the lighthouse to look up at Maggie, who was rolling paint high above the brunette on her broom. The witch circled around the building while a few other brushes, enchanted, painted everywhere else. It only took an hour or so for Maggie and her magic to paint the rest of the building, where normally it could have taken at least an entire day with pulleys and a crew.

Maggie floated down to Bea as she rested in the grass. She had paint on her pants and arms, but she looked satisfied. Maggie couldn't help but laugh a little; she was just as much of a mess as Bea was, even with her magic.

"Would you like a ride to the top?" Maggie asked.

Bea's eyes widened and she nodded. "Oh yes!" The chance to fly seemed to have been on her mind. Maybe she hadn't dared to ask due to a fear of being impolite?

Maggie sat with her broom between her legs and scooted up to give the other girl some room. Bea sat in the same manner and when she felt them rise, she held onto Maggie tightly for fear of falling. They flew to the top and landed on the platform around the light. Bea stepped off a little shakily but held onto the railing to look out at the view.

"Wow... It's gorgeous up here. That was amazing!" She turned to Maggie. "I'd never walk again if I knew how to do that." They both laughed.

The sun was setting on the ocean and the sound of the waves was a steady, comforting rhythm.

"Did you know my uncle?" Magnolia stepped up to the railing and leaned on it beside Bea.

"Canton and I used to play on these grounds when we were younger. Tom would play with us sometimes. He was great fun. When he wasn't taking care of the lighthouse, he'd be in town helping with repairs or just chatting with everyone. He was really outgoing and friendly. He liked to get into peoples affairs sometimes, though. Some people didn't like that, thought he was nosy and eccentric..." Bea laughed. "But I think he just really cared."

Maggie smiled sadly, wanting to laugh but just not having it in her. His death was still so recent. She looked out to the sea. "I only got to visit him a few times when I was younger. But we wrote letters back and forth until he died. I'm glad he lived such a happy life. I'm glad I get to walk in his shoes here."

Bea smiled sympathetically. "You'll do fine here. I'm sure you've already experienced the sour mood on magic, but I like you. Canton does, too."

"Why don't the people here like witches, anyway?"

"Well..." Bea looked down, watching the waves crash against the bluff. She seemed to want to be delicate, but honest. "A while ago, there used to be a witch who lived here. He helped improve the village, until he cast a spell on the fisheries. It poisoned almost the entire town. People died." Bea leaned into the railing. "We weren't all that keen on magic to begin with, Old Nan said it was too unpredictable. There hadn't been a witch here before then; his interference didn't help any in the end."

Magnolia blinked, suddenly frowning. She couldn't believe what she was hearing. A witch purposefully hurting others? That was something from the dark ages, not the present. "I can hardly believe it... Back home, that would never happen." She swelled with determination. "I'm going to change their minds."

"What do you mean?"

"About witches. I'll be useful... I'll help people. And I won't touch the fish." They both laughed.

Magnolia flew Bea back down to the lawn and saw her off. The lighthouse looked much improved and a feeling of accomplishment and pride washed over her. She poured herself a glass of lemonade and stood on her porch, looking up at the work she and Bea had done to the tall spire. It had been a long day, but happiness swelled within her. She had had fun, and she was sure Beatrice had, too. The lemonade was tart, but sweet on her tongue, and she laughed quietly to herself as she recounted the last few hours. She made her way back indoors, as the sun had disappeared beyond the horizon, and sat in front of the fire. Her eyes glanced over to the needles and thread on the coffee table and she thought that some magic would do well to finish those curtains after all.

CHAPTER TWO

Magnolia's morning consisted of fresh herbs from the garden steeped in hot water with honey and a mix of both hand and magic sewing. The new curtains were inviting and made the living area feel quite cozy. The redheaded witch felt a rush of excitement at the memories of yesterday. She had made new friends from the town, people who weren't afraid of her. She smiled as she thought of Mikel and what his reaction to her good news would be. Now she just had to convince the rest of the villagers that she was kind and trustworthy. She felt a sting of apprehension over it, but looking at her wand and broom sitting on the coffee table, she felt a wave of confidence rising once again.

She packed a bag, pocketed her wand, took her broom and headed out the front door, locking it behind her. She stuffed the key into her pants pocket before sitting on her broomstick and flying off the porch towards town.

It was a beautiful, warm and sunny day. People walked the streets, cleaning their walkways, shopping... It was pleasant and charming. As she landed in the street, glass quietly clinked together in her bag. The nearest person backed away and went into their house. She could hear the door locking behind them and saw them peek from behind the curtain in the nearest window. Maggie gave a sheepish, non-threatening smile and waved at them regardless. The curtain shut immediately.

"Oh, wow! You can fly?" A child ran up to her, cheeks flushed and hair frazzled. Maggie grinned and nodded.

"Yep!" She extended her broom to the girl. Little hands reached out to the wood and straw, but before she could so much as touch a bristle, her mother took her child by the wrist and pulled her away.

"That's dangerous!" the mother scolded. She gave Magnolia a scathing look and pulled her daughter down the street, away from the witch. The child whined and looked back at Maggie, who could only smile weakly and wave goodbye to the girl.

"This will be frustrating," Maggie mumbled to herself. She sighed and readjusted her bag over her shoulder before regaining some nerve. She had to start a business here if she wanted to afford living in Lightview. Having good relations with the people that took care of her uncle was the biggest step to getting there.

Walking through the village, Magnolia knocked on every door. Most didn't answer. Some slammed their doors in her face. There were a few polite declines, but so far, not a single person was interested in having a chat or looking at her wares.

Maggie made her way to the market square. She sat her bag down at Mikel's stand and sighed. The large man was wiping his hands on a rag when he saw her. He grinned widely.

"Well, hullo there, Miss Magnolia! What's brought you here with such a frown?"

Maggie lightly shook her bag, which slid the fabric down and revealed small bottles, jars, and other glass containers. They were filled with different colored liquids and bits of herbs. "I'm trying to get to know the villagers and let them try my potions. But so far, no one's wanted to talk to me. A lot have run away already."

Mikel scratched his beard and sat one hand upon his hip. He gave a small frown. "Aye, well... It's only the first day trying, lass." He stared at the containers on his table.

Maggie caught the look and took one of the jars out from her bag. It was filled with a muddy orange liquid, and sediment sat at the bottom. A smile came to her face then, even as she saw a look of apprehension come on Mikel's. She could tell he was concerned about her magic, just not as vehemently as everyone else.

"Have you been ill recently?" Maggie asked.

Mikel seemed to involuntarily flex his muscles and he gave a small smirk. "I don't get ill."

Maggie chuckled. "That's fair. You're in good shape, but here." She put the muddy drink on the table and pushed it towards the grocer. "The next time you come down with a cough, you'll probably be pretty tired. Drink this and you'll lose the cough, regain energy, and your cold will be cured."

Mikel picked the glass up, intrigued. "This is some kind of tea? Sorry, girl, but it looks...gross."

She laughed. "I call it fire tea. There's honey in it, so I think you'll like it. It'll give you a good kick, I promise."

Mikel swirled the jar, continuing to inspect the contents. He seemed to still be a little unsure, or maybe he felt like he wouldn't ever need it.

"Just take it for a rainy day. It's on me."

"Thanks, lass. I will. Y'know, that was a good pitch. Maybe keep the potions at home, though, until yer more settled with the townsfolk? Potions might be a bit intimidatin' for the others right now." Another sheepish smirk. He had been proof of that.

"You might be right... Thanks, Mikel." She pulled the bag over her potions and put it back over her shoulder. It was one thing to see someone use magic, and another to actually *consume* something with magic.

"Now, you can take this for the day. It'll keep those blues away." He handed her a bright red, vine-ripe tomato.

"Oh, it looks delicious. Thank you!" She waved goodbye with the tomato in hand and headed back out to the village streets.

~*~

Maggie decided to take a side street to the edge of town. The road overlooked a farm's vegetable fields and was separated by a deep drainage ditch. It hadn't rained in several days, so from where she walked she couldn't see any water, just mud. When she looked behind her towards the bay, she could see a stream that fed into the ocean.

She bit into the tomato Mikel had given her and juice dribbled down her chin. She chuckled quietly as she wiped it off. The tomato really was delicious, so flavorful and it hadn't even been grown with magic. Just as Mikel had predicted: it made her happy. Happy for the snack, and to have met Mikel and have his support.

Taking another bite, she saw someone further down the road pulling their bike out of the ditch. She watched him struggle as she got closer. No one else was around and she wondered if he needed some help.

"Are you alright?" she called. She ate the last of her fruit, wiped her mouth with the back of her hand and quickened her pace towards the stranger. He turned to look in her direction and Maggie realized it wasn't a stranger at all. She smiled with her recognition. "Canton?"

Canton's face flushed and he turned back to his bike, struggling to get it out and back onto the street. Maggie hadn't noticed it at first but now she could see he was covered in mud from falling in the ditch. He finally got the bike up and out as Maggie got near and she reached out to touch his forearm in concern.

"H-hey, Maggie, I'm okay," he assured her. He pushed

his glasses back up the bridge of his nose and seemed to find it difficult to look her in the eyes, so he looked down at his feet instead. He looked uncomfortable; his shoes were covered in mud, but Maggie could tell he was anxious, too—she knew all about that.

"Oh, no. Look, your bike is bent!" Maggie pulled out her wand and waved it at the front tire; the wheel was crooked and the spokes were close to breaking right off. Following Maggie's movements, it quickly bent back into its correct position and was suddenly good as new. She gave a satisfied look from her handiwork, smiling as she looked it over.

"Wow..." Canton held his face with one hand, looking a little shocked. "That was..." He struggled to find the words. "Thank you," he said finally. "I kind of lost control back there," he admitted, rubbing his neck.

"I imagine a bike can get away from you." Her smile widened. She had only ridden a bike a few times herself and wasn't so graceful, either. She looked Canton over, seeing the full extent of mud that still clung to his clothes. His shoes were simply caked now that she got a better look. They were likely to ruin if they were left that way for long. That wouldn't do.

Canton followed her gaze and went red all over. "It's not dung, it's just mud—no big deal—"

"Don't be silly." Maggie pointed her wand at Canton's feet and muttered a cleaning spell. The mud slid right off and went back into the ground. She did the same with his clothes.

Canton lifted one foot to examine it briefly. "You're really handy with that. Mud feels surprisingly heavy... Thank you."

"It's no problem at all." She was sure that would have helped with any embarrassment he might be feeling, but his face was still quite red. She hoped he didn't have a fever. "Are you sure the rest of you is alright? I have some tea if you're feeling under the weather," she offered. "Or if you've hurt your wrist, or any bones, I can help with that, too."

27

He shook his head quickly, causing his bangs to cover his eyes. He pushed them away and took a deep breath. "You make tea?" he managed.

"The base is tea, but they're a bit more potent than that. They're potions, actually." She wanted to ease into it, like Mikel had suggested, but she wouldn't deny what they were.

Canton and Maggie began to walk down the road together as they continued to talk. Canton walked his bike between them.

"What's the difference?" he asked.

"Well, tea is just water infused with plants," she explained. "Herbs and fungi, mostly. But a potion is with an infusion of magic. I make the tea more effective and can choose which properties to pull forward and which to eliminate completely, so long as I know what I'm working with." She smiled all the while; talking about her work made her happy.

Canton looked impressed, and that pleased her all the more.

"I can also turn some mighty strange things into a drinkable substance..." She lifted her hands eerily and watched Canton for his reaction. "Like stones, fairy wings, and animal guts!"

Canton stared at her. He seemed to be fighting with his expression, but Maggie could practically read his thoughts. Before he found his voice, Maggie laughed.

"I'm just teasing. I only work with plants." She elbowed her friend, who chuckled in return. His relief was palpable, and that made her feel a little bad, but it was all in good fun.

"I was about to say: I don't think I'd like to drink, er...eye of newt, or anything like that." Canton cracked a small smile.

Maggie looked surprised. She didn't think he'd have heard of that. "Eye of newt? Oh, I use that." She grinned suddenly. "That's just mustard seeds." She laughed and held onto the end of her braid playfully.

Canton laughed, too. "What, really? Just mustard seeds,

huh… That's something I'll have to tell Nan. She used to tell us all kinds of gross stories about witches." He gave her an apologetic look, probably hoping he hadn't offended her.

Maggie shrugged. "In my hometown, we'd get people visiting family and asking us all kinds of weird questions and ideas. I guess there just aren't that many witches around as I always thought there were. Living in a village of them will do that."

"Your whole town is full of witches?"

"Yep, mostly. Lots of families and extended families. I mean, anyone can choose to be a witch or not. It's hard work, though, and you need proper training. Some people just don't have the patience to learn how to channel their intention."

"Really? Even I could learn?" Canton readjusted his glasses, seemingly mystified at the idea of becoming a witch. He stopped right in the middle of the street.

"Oh, yes. I don't see why not!"

Some villagers passed them by and Canton looked worriedly after them, but Maggie didn't pay them any mind. He saw her watching him and cleared his throat. "Sorry. My grandmother, I don't approve of the way she treats you, but… I must admit, it's troubling to imagine how upset she'd be if she overheard this conversation."

The thought of losing a friend right after she'd gained one caused her to frown, but she recovered quickly. "It's not like you're running off to learn spells."

"No," he answered with a laugh. "But, w-well," he managed, and cleared his throat again, "Do you have any potions for arthritis?" He spoke loudly then and got a glance or two from passersby. Maggie liked Canton, even if he was a little awkward. She could be a bit awkward, though, too. What mattered was, he was kind, and thoughtful.

But the sudden interest in her wares was a surprise, and a good one at that. "I have just the thing," she said excitedly. After a moment of rummaging around in her bag, she pulled out a small vial. The glass reflected the light and was full of an auburn liquid with bright red berries.

"This is barberry," she said, handing him the vial. "Warm it up and pour it on a cloth to make a compress. It'll soak through the skin and heal the inflammation."

Canton took the vial. "Wow, this is actually better than I'd hoped." He handed her several folded bills from his pocket.

Maggie raised her hands and shook her head. "No, I couldn't possib—"

"Magnolia, please. Isn't this what you're out here doing?" He gestured at her bag and pushed the money at her again. She took it a little less reluctantly.

"Thank you."

Canton got onto his bike. "Thank *you*. Come by the store sometime." Maggie watched him ride away and disappear down a side street, back into town. She tightened her fist around the money he had given her, feeling grateful, and hopeful.

CHAPTER THREE

The store bell jingled as Canton stepped inside. He had locked his bike in the alley beneath the stairs rather than carry it up the side entrance to the apartment. Beatrice sat behind the counter and looked up at her brother with a frown. The store was empty; it was a slow afternoon, but it didn't stop Bea from feeling irritated.

"Canton! Where have you been?"

"I went for a ride down by the river." He rubbed the back of his neck; the movement had become a bit of a nervous habit, but this time it was just from stress. He looked down at himself only to be reminded that he wasn't covered in dirt or mud anymore. Maggie had taken care of that; he'd almost forgotten.

"I need to study and Dad made me work the register. Get over here already." Beatrice stood up from her stool.

"Sorry for that, but...do you know where Nana is?" Canton leaned against the counter, appearing hopeful.

Bea looked exasperated. "Why, so you two can argue again?"

Canton gave a soft laugh. "Actually, I have something for her." He pulled the vial from his pocket and handed it to his sister, who inspected it with curiosity. "Magnolia made it.

Can you give it to Nan? Help her warm it up and put it on a washcloth or something, then apply it to her wrists. Don't tell her where it came from yet…"

"Maggie did?" Bea stared at the vial with awe. She grinned, then, at what her brother was scheming. "You think this will help?"

"I think so. We'll see." He didn't have any reason not to trust Maggie or her magic, and he wanted his grandmother to not be so guarded just because Maggie was a witch. If this worked, it would help a lot more than just Old Nan's arthritis. That was his idea, anyway.

Bea looked impressed but she handed the vial back to her brother. "Sorry, Canton, but you'll have to do it. I've got to go!" She stepped out from behind the counter and ran upstairs without a second glance. Canton hadn't even had the time to protest. He sat down on the stool behind the counter and chuckled quietly to himself. Maybe it was better this way.

Customers had come and gone and the day seemed to drag on. Canton busied himself with dusting and rearranging stock when he heard footsteps from the apartment stairs. Old Nan steadied herself with the railing and her cane as she slowly made her way down, grumbling to herself about how her bones creaked.

"An old woman deserves better than stairs," Canton heard her say. He made his way over to her and offered his arm.

"It's not walking, child, it's climbing I can't stand." She pushed his arm away. "Be a dear and make a spot of tea for me. Your father's off on another run and your mother's no help when she's playing that piano." Canton smiled at his grandmother, knowing her moods all too well. He could hear the piano faintly through the ceiling and that made him smile, too. His mother was so fond of music; he was too, thanks to her.

"Sure, Nan. Let me get that for you." He made sure she made the walk to a nearby couch safely, despite her complaining that she could do it herself. Then he went to the back room to make the tea. While he heated the water, he took another kettle and heated the salve from the vial Magnolia had given him. The berries gave it a deep red color, but it turned almost pink as it was heated.

Once everything was finished, he set up a small platter with the tea and poured the salve on a cloth, which he placed beside the tea cup. It was more viscous than some salves he'd seen before, but it looked like it would apply on perfectly. Some of the barberries were still partially whole, but they were gelatinous enough to spread. It almost looked like jam, spread across the cloth as if it were bread.

"Here you are." Canton put the tray on a nearby table and handed her the tea cup.

"What is that?" Nothing got past Old Nan. She was eyeing the colorful, wet cloth with suspicion.

Canton reached out his hand. "Give me your arm, Nana. This is a salve I got today. It will help with the pain in your hands and arms."

"You think I'd let you put that on me? When we have a witch in town?" She sipped her tea with her eyes like daggers on that cloth.

"Nana, please... You don't need to worry. There's no spell cast on this." Not one that would cause any harm, anyway. At least, he hoped not. But he wouldn't ever get her to try if she knew it was Maggie's handiwork.

"You know how I feel about witches. Your grandfather died because of that awful man. We should have never let him in this town. I don't know *why* that Thomas was friends with him. It must have been his disgusting magic. A trick." She pursed her lips and looked away from her grandson, but still extended one hand to him. She got like this when she was upset, talking quickly and unwilling to listen. He was surprised when she gave her hand to him.

Canton pressed the cloth around Nan's hand and wrist. He heard her intake of breath and looked up to see her visibly relaxing.

"If Beatrice had been any younger, she could have died, too, you know." She took a long, relaxed breath. "Those poor children." She was watching Canton now and her expression softened. Her fingers flexed and she passed the tea cup to her covered hand. Canton moved the cloth to her other wrist. It hadn't left any berry residue like he'd thought it would.

"Are you feeling any better?" He didn't like thinking about what could have happened to Bea if she had eaten the poisoned fish from back then. He remembered full well the horrible event and counted himself and his family lucky for only losing one member of their family... He missed his grandfather dearly, but he didn't blame all witches like his Nana did. Only the one.

Old Nan mumbled something incoherent and Canton nudged her to speak up. She licked her lips and set the tea cup down on the tray. The skin on her hand that already had the treatment looked moist and slightly pink, but her fingers moved fluidly as she flexed them. She rolled her wrist and Canton saw tears come to her eyes.

"I've never felt such relief," she said quietly. "Did Doctor Jenkins give you this?"

Canton brushed the brown hair from his face and pushed his glasses against his nose before taking the cloth from her other wrist. She snatched the cloth back from him hastily and put it on the first wrist, as if to make sure the pain didn't come back. Canton smiled softly.

"Nan..." Her reaction was more than he could hope for, but he couldn't help but worry that she would be incredibly upset with him. Still, he needed to tell her. "Magnolia Hanna made this salve."

Old Nan stared at her grandson as if seeing him for the first time. Did she hear that correctly? Was she becoming senile in her old age? Her eyes narrowed before falling back to her wrists and how she held onto the damp cloth tightly. Her nostrils flared and then she exhaled slowly.

"Hanna, is it?" She pursed her lips at Canton and clicked

her tongue. "Tom's niece, then? I didn't realize he had such a capable witch in his family." She avoided her grandson's gaze by turning her head again. She had to know she had been unreasonably rude to the witch, and while she was too stubborn to normally admit it, he knew she couldn't deny the comfort she felt from using the salve. "We'll see if this lasts by morning." To say she was skeptical was the least of it, but this was a good start.

Canton almost sighed with relief. Instead, he nodded and collected the empty tea cup and tray. When he came back from the kitchen, he saw Nan applying the cloth to her legs. He smiled again but said nothing. She must have been feeling great relief, since she wasn't scolding him for tricking her. But he hadn't done it to hurt or worry her... He figured she knew that. He decided to close up shop for the rest of the day; they were slow, anyway.

~*~

The young man in the window brushed his hair away from his glasses before adjusting the display. He had an attention for detail and this particular display was slightly askew. He clasped his hands together and stood back to look at his work. It had been a few days since he gave his grandmother the salve and things had been quiet lately.

"Perfect." Smiling, he picked up his step stool when he noticed the witch through the window. He dropped the stool in surprise, barely missing his toes. The clamor earned him a holler from deeper within the store.

"Sorry!" Canton went to pick up the stool once more, but watched as the redhead moved further down the street, a cat at her heels and flowers in her hair. He looked down at himself in a pondering manner before carrying the stool quickly into the back and grabbing something from off the shelf.

"Back in a minute!" He could hear his grandmother

knocking her cane against the counter even as the bell rang on his way out.

An audible meow caused Magnolia to look behind her at the black cat.

"I didn't realize you were following me." She smiled and kneeled down to pet its head. "Do you belong to anyone, I wonder?" The cat purred and rubbed its head against Magnolia's knee.

Canton was a standing stone in the middle of the street. He thought she had seen him and he was embarrassed to have been seen so soon. Realizing she hadn't noticed him yet, he sighed in relief. She was preoccupied with the cat, so she hadn't seen him rushing out to meet her. Finding his nerve, he made his way over to her, more casually than before.

"Magnolia?"

Maggie looked up to see her new friend. He shakily handed a can to her, which she took.

"Hello, Canton. What's this?" She turned the can over in her hands before reading the label. She grinned and Canton felt his ears go warm. "Cat food? And just in time." She pulled her wand out from her pocket and used it to open the can. The lid rolled back easily and the cat at her feet mewled at the scent of fish. She sat it down for the sweet creature to eat.

Canton silently berated himself for forgetting a can opener, but it obviously wasn't necessary with Maggie's magic.

"She certainly likes it," he managed.

"Oh, does she belong to you?"

Canton shook his head. "Oh, no. She's a regular, though." He watched as the black cat happily ate, her tail wrapping around her body in pleasure as she sat. She didn't seem bothered by them, nor the people walking by on the street. Only an ear twitched every so often.

"Her name's Tempest. My sister and I found her after a bad storm. We nursed her back to health and she's hung around ever since."

Maggie grinned. "How lucky!" She kneeled down to pet Tempest, scratching under her chin. "You'll bring good fortune to the whole town," she told the purring thing.

"My grandmother loved the salve," Canton said suddenly. "She doesn't feel the pain in her arms at all anymore and it's reduced a lot in her legs."

Maggie looked up, surprised. "She used it?" She stood quickly, grinning. "That's fantastic! I'm so happy for her. I can make more for her legs. She shouldn't feel it at all anymore after that."

"That would be great, actually. She'll be happy to walk up and down stairs again without any complaints." He found himself reaching for Maggie's hand and held it tightly. The sudden grasp of affection surprised him, but he couldn't help himself. There was warmth there, and it wasn't just the blood pumping through her hand, but actual, true kindness. All it took was a salve to soften her grandmother. Maggie had done that. "Thank you so much. I think she's starting to realize you're not the same as that witch from ten years ago... She's still uncomfortable, but you don't have to worry about her when you come into the store again."

Maggie squeezed Canton's hand in return, and tears stung her eyes. She blinked to clear them and grinned. "Oh please, it's the least I can do," she said, blushing from the praise. "But what a milestone! Old Nan wasn't exactly subtle about her dislike for me... The fact that you think she's turning a new leaf means a lot." She took her hands from Canton, then.

"How about we have lunch to celebrate?" she offered. Rummaging into her bag, she pulled out a sandwich, which was wrapped in a translucent paper. She waved it enticingly and smiled that same, heartfelt smile.

Looking back at his family's shop, Canton fiddled his thumbs together, but thought quickly. "I'd love to," he replied. But despite his earnest answer, he still felt a little nervous; if he asked his nan she'd surely tell him no. So, better not to ask at all. He'd have to learn to stop seeking her approval, then. "Where did you have in mind?"

"Follow me." Maggie's excitement was intoxicating. She led him down the alley beside his shop and stopped abruptly, turning around to face him. Reaching down to her belt, Canton came to realize exactly what he'd gotten himself into. She was getting bolder.

Her broom sat suspended in air between them both and Maggie looked from it to her friend with dark, playful eyes. "There's this tree at the cliffside outside the cemetery..." She smiled sheepishly. "I know it sounds silly, but it looks like such a nice place for a picnic. And besides, I thought you might like to try flying?" Her brow rose as she asked, playing her innocence. Bea had been so excited to fly, maybe she assumed he would too.

But Canton was not excited. He gave a nervous chuckle and stared at the broom as if it were about to catch on fire. Not wanting to appear afraid, though, he forced a grin. "Y-yeah... I've never seen anyone fly before, though. How does it work?" Bea had told him the whole story, so he was stalling, but maybe hearing it from the witch herself would ease his fears.

As excited as she was, she still seemed to sense the storekeeper's apprehension. She smiled sympathetically. "It's really easy. Just hold on to me and I'll do all the work." She lifted her leg over the broomstick and loosely gripped the handle. There was plenty of room for Canton to sit behind her, and while he was tentative to do so, he took a seat. He wanted to know what flying felt like, and he didn't want to tell Maggie no. But it didn't stop his anxiety. As their feet left the ground, Canton immediately tightened his grip around Maggie and she laugh-coughed in surprise as the wind was almost knocked away from her.

"Relax, if you can. We'll be there soon," she reassured him.

Canton's home rushed out beneath them, along with his

entire village. He tried closing his eyes but they wouldn't stay shut, and while his body shook in fear, he couldn't help but feel awed at the smallness of everything so high up. *We're like birds,* he thought, feeling the breeze rush through his hair and clothes.

His grip loosened some as they hovered above the town, floating still for the time being, allowing Canton the time to take in his surroundings. Maggie was watching his expression from around her shoulder, and when she felt like he was ready, she soared at a comfortable pace towards the cemetery.

Once they were over the graveyard, it was as if the graves weren't even there. Camphor trees shielded them from Maggie and Canton's view. A few could be seen through thinner foliage until they were beyond the fence and at the cliffside.

A final, lone camphor tree sat close to the edge and shaded them from the sun as they landed beneath it. Canton held on to Maggie in full force once more as the breeze from the ocean pushed at them.

"Did you enjoy it?" Maggie asked, and laughed. Canton stiffly released his grip from around her waist and somehow managed to get off the broom. He collapsed onto his bottom near the foot of the tree, his glasses askew. For a moment, he didn't speak, so Maggie took the time to sit her broom against the trunk of the tree.

"Yes," he finally said. "And no. That was really scary." His hands had stopped shaking, though, and he was adjusting his glasses when he started to laugh. It made Maggie laugh, too, and they were both sitting in the grass laughing with the wind from the sea.

It was a gloriously warm day made perfect by the constant breeze, and the shade of the tree made it all the more comfortable. As their laughter subsided, Canton fell onto his back and sprawled his limbs out in the grass with a sigh. "It's wonderful to be outside of the village, even if it's not very far. Do you go flying often? It's exhilarating, but still pretty scary..."

"I've been trying to keep a low profile, you know, as a witch and all. But flying is my favorite thing to do besides making potions...and eating." She giggled.

Maggie spread out a cloth between them with a sandwich on either side, the crinkled paper waving in the breeze beneath the weight of bread. She sat with her legs beside her and took a bite of her sandwich. "I packed extra," she said between bites, "since I wasn't sure how long I'd be out today. I thought I'd sell more potions... But it's still not looking so good."

Canton watched the redhead and smiled. "You'll get there, Maggie... Your salve did amazing work. They just need to give you a chance." He rolled onto his side and took the other sandwich, supporting himself with his elbow. "Anyway, I don't think a single person in this town doesn't know of you. Maybe not showing much of your magic right now is for the best. I wouldn't have been able to get Nana to drink a potion, but the salve was pretty easy to win her over."

He took a bite of his sandwich before continuing. "The witch that used to live here...he used to flaunt his magic all the time. Rubbed it in the villagers' faces, from what Nan tells us. It didn't really scare the villagers so much until it hurt someone. Now they don't seem to trust any of it, even if some of our workings are still magically maintained."

"You have magic-run equipment here?" The surprise was plain on her face, but Canton didn't blame her for sounding a little dubious.

"Yeah." He took another bite; it was so tasty, some kind of thick, creamy substance on oat bread with white meat. Chicken, maybe. "Half our electricity runs off magic. Once it was set up, we couldn't undo it...and it's saved us in a few storms, so you don't hear anyone complaining." He hummed to himself at that. "We have a desalination pump that runs off magic, too. Saves a lot of power and runs much faster than the pump in Westdown. The only thing they were able to stop the magic on was the fishery. It was just a single boat, but it didn't need anyone to man it. The town destroyed it. I don't blame them, though... We don't want any magic near the fish again, after what happened.. Some things are just better done by hand, I guess." He gave a sheepish smile. "No offense, of course."

Maggie shook her head. "None taken. Even as a witch, I can understand the importance of doing things with your hands, as opposed to your wand." The horns of several boats went off below the cliff. Maggie watched as they lay anchor, and some sailed into the port to unload. "Still, that's amazing. I had no idea there was any magic left, or even any at all."

"They don't like to admit it, but they know it's useful. So you really haven't sold any of your potions yet?"

"Besides to you?" She shook her head. "No, sadly. I'll get some good luck sooner or later, though. Like you said, they just need to see my potions in action."

"That's the spirit." Canton grinned." I'll spread the word, and once Nan gets more comfortable, maybe I can get her to talk about your salve. I might even be able to sell some from the shop, if you wanted..." Granted, he had no idea if his parents would go for it.

A loud, wet cough sounded behind them and they both looked around in surprise.

"You kids better not be castin' spells on my grounds." An old man with a shovel over his shoulder walked towards them. "Is that you, Canton? Wot're you doin' flyin' over here? You a witch now?" Wiry eyebrows narrowed at Maggie and back at Canton.

"Oh, Pete, you scared me." Canton got to his feet and brushed off his pants before shaking the old man's hand. Old Pete ran his fingers through his beard and coughed again. He spat phlegm into the grass, but managed a wrinkled smile. Canton smiled sheepishly and gestured to Maggie.

"This is Magnolia. Maggie, this is Old Pete, the groundskeeper for the cemetery. And, well...the gravedigger, too." Old Pete gave another wet cough after Canton's introduction.

"You the witch I'm hearin' about?" Old Pete looked her up and down and Maggie got to her feet as she was addressed.

"I think I'm the only one," she said, not unkindly. Old Pete laughed at that. He spit into the grass again. "I've got a pretty nasty cough, girl. As if you couldn't tell. I can't stand it. I hear yer goin' around sellin' potions. What can you do for an old man?"

Maggie was taken by surprise; she clearly hadn't expected him to ask her for her business. She fished into her bag, glass clinking lightly, and pulled out a jar.

"I've got a bad hip, too," he added, staring at the jar in her hand.

The witch pulled out a vial of blue liquid and handed that and the jar to Old Pete. "This is fire tea, and this is a bone tincture. You can drink the tea at any time, but you should drink the tincture before bed, after a meal."

Old Pete took the potions and handed her a few bills and coin. Even on his old, cracked face, they could see a smile. "Thanks, girl. I'll let you know how it goes. Don't be castin' any strange spells on my hedgerows now."

"Please do! And I won't!" Maggie was beaming. Canton gave her a thumbs up of encouragement.

The gravedigger stalked off back to his cemetery and Maggie started to giggle, beside herself in excitement. "How great is that! You and Old Pete, my first sales... I better make more fire tea." They grinned and packed up their lunch before walking back into town; Canton did enjoy the flight but he felt more comfortable if he tried again at another time. Maggie didn't mind, saying she enjoyed walking around the village and familiarizing herself with the streets.

CHAPTER FOUR

A lanky, dark haired witch was lifting lumber, his cheeks flushed both in effort and in embarrassment. He pushed the two by four up against the frame of the building with a muffled *umph!* and wiped the sweat from his face with his forearm. Readjusting his rolled sleeves, he wiped his hands together and set them on his hips, feeling rather proud of himself.

"First time at manual labor, huh?" Tom tipped his farm hat at the witch and winked.

"N-n-no! O-of course not!" Basil dropped his hands to his sides in balled fists, hiding the lack of muscles and trying to look tough. Tom laughed.

"Let me see those." Tom, the embodiment of muscles themselves, took Basil's hands in his own rough digits, engulfing them like a stone in quicksand. "Soft as a baby's bottom," Tom remarked. He barked with laughter and smacked the witch on the back; a friendly gesticulation that almost knocked the poor witch over.

Basil's face was as red as ever, as Tom had taken one of his hands again and fished out bandages from his pocket. He wrapped up the blisters on Basil's hands and then patted them gently.

"Gloves, Basil." Another wink.

"Or magic?" A challenging glower.

"Gahaha!" Tom almost smacked Basil on the back again, if not for the fright in the other man's eyes at the prospect. His raised hand moved back to scratch the back of his head; a smooth save. "Ah, Basil, this is good for you." He lifted a piece of lumber up over his head, grinning from ear to ear. He handed it off to a nearby worker, who carried it almost as easily to where it belonged within the structure. "Maybe stick with magic, though. That's fine. We'll get things done faster!"

"It'd be even quicker if you all used magic, but I suppose I can't expect that out of a podunk town like this." Basil looked up wearily to the roof trusses being erected. The villagers gave Basil no heed and continued to work diligently despite his glare.

Tom smiled. "Hard work, sweat n' tears. And laughter, of course! That's Lightview's way." He laughed again.

There was something about Tom's constant positivity. It drew Basil in, in spite of himself. He swallowed his pride and retrieved his wand from his pocket. The elegant, dark wood reflected the hot summer sun and seemed to sing. Basil's apprehension melted away. He directed his wand at a hammer and nails and stepped into the structure to assist a woman putting up a partition wall, the tools floating beside him.

"That's the way." Tom gave a thumbs up and returned to sawing lumber.

The town had been welcoming to Tom when he had arrived; he'd already been living in Lightview for several years. When Basil had arrived, they were just as welcoming...albeit a little concerned with his magic that they were so very unfamiliar with. When finding how useful it was in improving the town, they embraced him well enough. They had already changed the desalination pump to be powered by magic, and they were talking about electricity next. Tom wondered if his lighthouse would one day be powered by magic, too. He had chuckled at the idea, though. The lighthouse was his baby; he said he'd rather run it on his own.

He didn't understand Basil all the time, but he tolerated the man more than most. Basil had a way about him... He was a little rough around the edges, so to speak. He complained a lot, he was judgmental, and he liked to say he was better than others because of his magic. But Tom could see something in the man most of the other villagers couldn't. He just wasn't sure what it was yet.

~*~

It had been a long working day and Basil was beat. With a heavy hand, he wiped his hair from his face and stood back to see the building they'd raised. He may not have done much lifting or other manual labor with his own hands, but magic still took its toll and it was as hot as fire that afternoon. The building was...kind of wonderful, actually. Basil had never built anything before, and while it was unfinished, it already had a nice sort of charm to it.

"Great job, everyone," the villagers told each other. They shook hands, clapped each other on the back and started to head home for the day. Tom stepped behind Basil and whistled, impressed.

"How do you like it?" he asked the witch.

"It's okay." Basil shrugged. That he couldn't fully express himself was infuriating, but he didn't want anyone to know he actually *liked* having helped. Though, to be honest, he did kind of hate it at the same time. For the most part, he felt people should learn to help themselves. Why did he have to show them how it was done? Magic was the most useful skill in the world. But he liked showing off and sometimes, when he was actually listening, being thanked was kind of nice, too.

Tom guffawed. "Just okay, huh? Well, it'll be done soon.

Maybe you'll appreciate it then. Let's go grab some dinner. Are you staying somewhere nearby?" He wasn't sure Basil had the funds for an inn, and Tom assumed he didn't have any friends that would take him in, from what he knew about the man. Where he had been sleeping since he arrived, Tom had no idea. But, he didn't judge. Maybe he'd lighten up with some friendly company.

Basil chewed the inside of his lip as he considered. "I have a camp just outside of town...but a meal would be nice, sure. I-I can pay," he added hastily.

"That won't do. Come on, then."

Tom led Basil through the market square and down the main street. Basil kept expecting to stop at one of the cafes or restaurants, but eventually there were only residences, and before he knew it, there was nothing but open field.

"Where are we going?" For a brief moment, he wondered if Thomas was tricking him, and his mind began to fester with dark thoughts. He didn't have any of his gear and leaving town without it made him uncomfortable. Thankfully, he had his camp cloaked, but it didn't help his current position. Still, he guessed if he had to defend himself, he could. He did still have his wand, and that was all he needed in a pinch.

"I have a roast, and I can't very well eat it alone. You can stay the night on my couch, if you want. They say it'll be cold tonight, and I've got a nice fire." Tom pointed to the lighthouse at the end of the peninsula. The sun was setting and the lighthouse shined on in the dim, warming Basil's thoughts along with the light breeze that swept in.

Whatever it was Tom might have been insinuating, Basil was at first suspicious. It wasn't like the witch to be very trusting, and the idea that Tom was as sincere as he sounded was hard to grasp. He stopped walking and almost turned around, but Tom still walked on, confident and straightforward as ever.

Basil stared after him for a moment, gripping his shirt

with uncertainty, and the grass caressed his legs from the sea breeze. His warming thoughts had cooled, but Tom's steady pace seemed to keep them from falling back into the dark. Basil picked up his pace again and trailed behind the man, his eyes going back between the ground and Tom's back, wondering.

They walked the rest of the way in silence—that is, they weren't speaking. Tom was whistling, sometimes humming, and running his hands along the tall grass that grew beside the path that led to his home. Basil couldn't see it, but he could tell the man was smiling. It was in his gait; maybe it was in his entire being. To the witch, the man seemed to glow before him in the setting sun. It made his eyes sting with tears; he rubbed them with irritation and averted them back to the grass. He was staring at wildflowers and smelling lavender when he heard footsteps on wood. Looking up, Tom was creaking open the screen door to the lighthouse and unlocking the front door.

"Home sweet home." Tom smiled.

Upon entering Tom's home, Basil caught sight of an unlit hearth, a comfortable, worn couch, wooden beams along the ceiling and the entrance to, what appeared to be, a kitchen. Despite how chilly it was in the dark home, it *felt* warm.

Tom was kneeling at the hearth preparing some wood when Basil stepped up behind him with his wand. "Let me." Basil pointed the wand at the fireplace, shooting fire in the form of a small ball, lighting the kindling aflame.

"Why, thank you! That's much quicker." Tom wiped his hands on his pants.

Basil shrugged and eyed a picture frame on the mantelpiece, facing down. He reached for it, but Tom held it down, causing the witch to recoil in surprise.

"Sorry." Tom smiled again, but this time it didn't meet his eyes. A sad smile, Basil thought. He knew those well. "Looking at this just...makes me a bit lonely." He stepped away from the hearth and took the picture with him as he headed into the kitchen to stoke the oven. "Feel free to make yourself at home," he called. "There's a blanket by the bookcase if you're a bit chill."

Basil rubbed his arms to warm them, despite the fire. Looking around, he saw the bookcase in the corner. There weren't many books there, not compared to Basil's old study. Without glancing at the titles, he wrinkled his nose at the case and picked up the blanket on the chair beside it. He shivered into it and tightened the fabric around him; it was colder on the other side of Tom's living room. He could hear Tom cutting vegetables across the house and glanced at the light coming from the kitchen, but took one final look at the bookcase.

Despite how small Tom's library was, each book looked well-read. The spines were creased, but it appeared they were well cared for. They weren't falling apart yet. Fresh and dried flowers sat in the empty spaces on the case and small stones sat here and there like knickknacks.

The walls had nails installed for pictures, but no picture hung on any of them. For once, Basil thought of someone other than himself and he wondered if the picture on the mantel, as well as the ones missing from the wall, were of his family. By the way Tom had reacted, he assumed they were dead. He decided it was best not to inquire so as to avoid an awkward and difficult conversation.

Tom was humming to himself as he loaded the oven and Basil walked into the kitchen, looking apprehensive. Tom noticed him and raised a brow. Then, of course, he smiled. The warmth returned.

"So, Basil! How are you settling into Lightview?"

"It's not so bad. Everyone seems...okay. It's frustrating that no one uses magic here, but I guess that's why they need me." He stared at the table, knowing he was being arrogant, but refusing to meet Tom's eyes.

Tom put one hand on his hip and cocked a brow at the witch. He decided to ignore the man's attitude, and his expression still didn't change. "Well, you've already done quite a bit to help us out. The mayor's pretty pleased he won't have to worry about his power failing in a storm again."

"We'll have to have a storm to really test that. It's not done yet, anyway." Basil fingered circles into the countertop and shrugged the blanket away from his neck. It was much warmer in the kitchen; he'd probably just take it off soon enough.

"I don't have any doubts," Tom replied. "How about you look into something else you can help improve on the town? Maybe if you help out enough, some villagers might want to learn magic from you? Then you wouldn't be the only witch."

Basil hadn't ever thought of teaching before, at least not to the villagers here. As if they'd want his help...

"You think so?" His eyes met Tom's and the older man nodded. Cheeks reddening, Basil looked down at the counter again.

Tom reached into the fridge and pulled out a couple of beers. He popped off the caps of each and set one in front of Basil.

"If you don't want to teach, I'm sure there's something else you can do to help someone."

"Yeah... I was thinking that, too." They clinked their glasses together and Basil finally smiled. "I knew it was a good idea." Ever arrogant, but Tom couldn't help but encourage him with a smile of his own. Helping someone, even being nice to someone, would do Basil good.

~*~

A crowd had gathered at the mayor's home just as the sun was setting beyond the horizon. It was darker than usual, because the power in that area of town had been shut off. Some of the villagers had looks of irritation, others of genuine interest. They knew Basil had shut the power off for a reason, and a few were openly skeptical over the idea of electricity without a typical power source.

Basil stood at the top of the steps, his back to them. He wasn't listening to the comments or whispers, which he assumed were of derision. From the villagers' initial negative response to his arrival, he still just imagined they wouldn't have anything productive to say.

Slowly, he guided his wand above his head in an arc and lights began to switch on one by one in the mayor's building. Then, they started to turn on quicker on the rest of the block. By the end of it, Basil was sweating and breathing deep, but he had a self-satisfied smirk on his face.

The mayor shook Basil's hand before raising his arms in gesture of his building. "We'll always have a way of contact now. We don't have to fear a storm disconnecting us again. This is grand work, Basil!"

The witch shrugged and as the villagers crowded around the mayor, he slipped away from the throng. He hadn't realized the villagers had wanted to speak with him, or if he had, he pointedly ignored them. If there was any praise, he just assumed it was forced. He was starting to wonder why he had bothered to help the town anyway.

Tom was at the docks, staring out at the fishery. He had just said goodbye to an associate when he heard someone else walking by.

"Well hello there, Basil. Working hard?" He smiled.

Normally Basil would have taken that as an attack on his person, but he had learned Tom just wasn't the type, and while his skin seemed to bristle in reaction, he was able to swallow that feeling. "Yes, actually. I'm done now, though."

"I'm hearing a lot about you lately, you know." Tom turned and crossed his arms, almost in an accusatory fashion. But still, he looked pleased.

Basil raised a brow in suspicion and took a half step back. "What would anyone have to say about *me?*"

"Well, that you've been very helpful. People have been talking all day about how you're revolutionizing power." He didn't mention the criticism, but that was neither here nor there. Most of it had become positive, as Basil was proving himself to be a useful person despite his grumblings.

"I hadn't even done anything yet...not until just now." Basil rubbed his arm self-consciously and looked away. Maybe the villagers *had* really wanted to talk to him, and not just to say something negative, like he had assumed.

"Word travels fast in a podunk town like this." Tom winked.

Using my own words, Basil thought. He smiled faintly. "I see... Well, I just figured it was about time you all started using something more sophisticated and reliable." It was Basil's turn to cross his arms. "Living by the sea is nice and all, but you're not properly prepared for the long term."

"Oh?" Tom suddenly laughed. "So you know more about the sea than we do, hm?" He rustled Basil's hair and put an arm around him, leading him away from the fishery. "You're the talk of the town and you still haven't noticed."

"I don't really listen to anyone," Basil muttered. That was partly true. He certainly listened to Tom. They had become good friends at this point, at least Basil thought so. He assumed Tom felt the same way.

He did. It was one of the few times Basil was correct in his assumption, as most of his assumptions were negative, self-defeating mind-reading. Except, of course, when he was acting like a true git. Still, Tom couldn't blame him for how he felt. While Tom wasn't keen on assuming himself, he thought it safe to assume Basil had gone through some rough times, wherever he was from. He liked to give chances. Everyone deserved them.

Sometimes, many.

51

CHAPTER FIVE

Maggie wiped the sweat from her brow with her forearm as the other hand firmly held to her wand, which was being used to hold lumber in place on the roof of a neighbor's building with her magic. It was nearing the end of summer, but that meant for incredibly hot afternoons like this one. Nolan, the man she was assisting, was fixing a hole that made for a nasty leak in the late summer rains.

"Instead of a potion, you can cure my headaches by helping with this leak," he had said, laughing.

So, that was what they were doing now. Hammering away and reapplying shingles. When the repair was finished, Nolan stood up and wiped his hands together with a grin. "That was a great help, Miss Magnolia. I'm glad I requested you." He went to shake her hand and slipped on a spare piece of shingle. Shouting and flailing his arms, he went flying down the roof.

His wife cried in alarm from the street below and Maggie, her expression shocked, managed to cast out a levitation spell just as Nolan flew off the roof. Relieved, she slowly lowered him down to the street.

Nolan barked with laughter, all while his wife yelled at him for being careless. Maggie picked up the remnants of tools and materials and then flew down to Nolan and Rebecca on her broomstick.

"That was a close call, Maggie!" Nolan cheered.

"You're telling me." She chuckled. "Please be more careful, though."

"I owe you another thanks for saving my skin back there." He managed his handshake then and gave a hearty grin to go with it. Maggie beamed both in pride and satisfaction, for having been of use and having prevented a nasty fall. She liked the Peters; while Rebecca was known for being loudly concerned about things, she meant well and would have been devastated if anything had befallen her husband.

"Thanks isn't needed for preventing a broken neck. I'll help anytime."

"You come on back around sometime and we'll fix you up a nice supper," said Rebecca, and she hugged Maggie tightly.

Maggie had been doing rather well the last month. Ever since she'd cured Old Nan's arthritis, the old woman had been spreading praises high and low in Lightview. The turn around in her attitude was a welcome surprise, but every once in a while, she still gave the witch a hard time. Maggie found it to be something like tough love and didn't take it personally anymore. She was getting more requests and was even starting to get them from Westdown, the next town over.

"In case your husband bothers your nerves, take this." Maggie took from her pocket a small potion. "It's like a full body massage in a vial. It's very relaxing."

Rebecca kissed Maggie on the cheek. "You are so sweet! Thank you, doll. I know I'll be needing it soon." And they laughed. Nolan was a good man but he was very excitable and a bit clumsy. With a baby on the way, she needed all the relaxation she could get.

Maggie was on her way to meet Mikel and Prairie in the market when she ran into Canton and Beatrice in front of their family's store.

"How are you?" Maggie hugged them both as they shared pleasantries. "I'm going to the market square if you'd like to come. Mikel wants to talk about the Harvest Festival."

"Oh, that's coming up soon! I almost forgot. I can't believe it's here already." Bea smiled widely as she thought on past festivals fondly. "We'd love to go; Mikel always has something fun planned."

The three headed down to the market where Mikel and Prairie were setting out a spread on a picnic table behind their stand. The market wasn't very busy today; the heat had driven most of them off. Luckily for Mikel, his stand had a nice shade cover, and it covered the picnic table, too. In the shade, every breeze that came through was put to good use in cooling them down.

"Ah, you brought the siblings. The more the merrier." Mikel gave his signature, hearty laugh and handed them a piece of watermelon from his table spread.

"Come and have a seat," Prairie called and patted the table. Maggie and Bea sat across from Prairie, while Mikel and Canton stood. Canton was eyeing the produce, thinking of a meal plan for later while he ate his watermelon.

"The Harvest Festival is coming up soon, lass, and as a new villager here in Lightview, I'd like to be the first to tell you all about it."

"Oh, it's so fun, Maggie! You'll love it." Bea nudged her friend in the shoulder and Mikel gave her a sardonic scowl at the interruption, only to slip back into another smile.

"The wife and I are helping the Williams' farm set up a corn maze for the day. The market will be full of seasonal dishes and treats, there will be music, and at night the fishermen set up lights on their boats and we'll set off fireworks. The point, lass, of the festival—aside from having fun, of course—is to honor the harvest."

"Naturally," Maggie piped in.

"Naturally," Mikel agreed. "And that's not just the

greenery, lass. But the fisheries, too, and all the good fortune we've had here in Lightview. It's been a good year, though we thought things would get a bit shady and unfortunate after that Basil fellow came knockin' on our doors again the day our Thomas died... It was a damn shame, and bad luck, too."

Maggie's smile faded and she looked around at her company with uncertainty. "Basil?" she inquired. It did sound like bad luck; she still thought of her uncle often and when she was alone, found herself weeping over his death. It was a hard knock to take. But she was glad the village was mostly business as usual.

"Oh, aye." Prairie reached across the table to hold Maggie's hand. She gave it a tight squeeze. "Basil's the witch everyone here's so afraid of. He lived among us, not ten years past, and he seemed a decent fellow...I suppose."

"You hated him, dear. No use in pretenses now." Mikel sat heavily at the picnic table.

"Oh, he was a nasty lout. No appreciation for hard work, always had something negative to say. I didn't like him, not at first, but it wasn't until he killed old Jonas and those children that I couldn't stand the thought of him."

"What?" Maggie exclaimed. She looked between Bea and Canton.

"Oh, he didn't kill anyone directly," Bea corrected.

"Not that we know," Canton replied quietly.

"He ran away as soon as old Jonas died. That's your grandfather, girl," Prairie chided Beatrice.

Bea averted her gaze, frowning. She didn't like being reminded of her grandfather's death.

"Why did he come back?" Maggie asked Mikel.

"He gave a sorry excuse for an apology and acted as though he wanted to move back in. But we chased him right back out of town. Ten years, he'd been gone. We never thought we'd see him again. Most of the folk here were scared out of their britches. But they wanted blood, too, if they could manage it. Thankfully, it didn't come to that."

"You'd defend him?" Prairie furrowed her brow at her husband.

"Dear, that man is plum powerful. He floated in here like a ghost and disappeared without a trace. He cast fire down upon us, like a rain from hell." Maggie could see goosebumps on Mikel's large arms and felt a shiver down her own spine. "None of us could hope to fight against a man like that."

"He's no man," Prairie muttered.

"Aye," Mikel agreed. "So, no. We don't need any more deaths in Lightview if we can help it."

~*~

"Looks the same as it ever did."

A man stood at the top of a hill and gazed down upon the village below. The village of Lightview, the town he had finally grown to love after having taken it for granted for such a long time. Smoke rose from the chimneys and he watched as a ship departed from the port. He managed a tight smile as he remembered the fishery disaster. Basil readjusted his grip on his travel pack and floated down towards town, his feet merely inches above the surface and with no broom in sight.

A young man chopping wood just outside of the village's entrance looked up to see Basil floating towards him. Even without seeing Basil's face, he knew who it was and his face went pale. He dropped his axe in fear, though Basil didn't recognize it as such, and the man ran into the village with great haste.

As Basil reached the archway, he heard the alarm bell ring. He gave a quizzical look at his surroundings; clearly this was a welcoming? It had been ten years since he'd been to Lightview. He'd been of so much help then, why not now? Surely, they couldn't still be mad—

"Damn!" Something hit him on the forehead. He watched the rock tumble beneath his feet and reached up to feel blood dripping down his brow.

"What'd you come back for?! To finish us off?" It was the Guard. They weren't a big presence in town, because they didn't need to be, but every town needed a sense of safety.

Basil licked two fingers and brushed them across his wound. The cut was suddenly gone. He wiped the blood away with a handkerchief as several more villagers joined the guardsmen. His patience was already growing thin, but he steadied his breathing. He must be able to reason with them.

"I came back to apologize," Basil began. "I want to live among you all again. I'm much stronger now, wiser!" He gestured to his floating figure, but the villagers just stared in shock and disgusted awe. He didn't understand their expressions; he had *learned* from his mistake, surely they could see that?

"Spare me. We don't need a witch living here again. You killed enough of us; can't you see we don't want you here?"

"I can help you!" He began to grind his teeth, his anger rising again. "I can—"

"We don't want your help!" Another stone was thrown, hitting Basil beneath one eye.

"Agh!" Basil threw his arms out, sending out a wave of fire. Flames licked at their clothes and singed some of the villagers, but went out almost immediately. The witch floated himself quickly over their heads and away. If anyone would understand him, it would be Tom. He had disappeared in a flash and the villagers, scared and making sure they weren't hurt, hadn't even seen the witch go. They checked each other's wounds and scratched their heads shakily, almost believing they'd seen a ghost.

"Tom!" Basil banged his fist on the lighthouse door. He looked behind himself to see if he had been followed, despite knowing he had been too quick for them to have caught up, or even seen where he'd fled to. He was grounded now and he felt incredibly heavy standing there at Tom's doorstep. But it was more than just the weight of himself that burdened him.

Like the rest of the village, Tom's lighthouse was unchanged, if not for the faded paint upon the tall pillar of light. The wildflowers were all there, beautifully beaming in the spring sunshine and swaying in the ever-present sea breeze. They mocked him. The door opened and there was Tom. His expression was that of surprise.

"Basil?" His surprise turned to a smile and then quickly faded at the frantic look on the witch's face. He saw another cut under Basil's eye that the witch had forgotten to heal. Basil pushed him aside—in his own home—and let himself in.

"Tom, how can you stand it?" Basil whirled around to confront his friend. His arms were spread out wide, almost accusatory. "These people are crazy, they attacked me!"

"Ha, what? Crazy's a strong word…" Tom wasn't sure what had come over Basil; he'd never seen the witch this frantic before, and to show up so suddenly after ten years… "They're fine folk, Basil, but your magic inadvertently *killed* members of their families. You poisoned the food supply. People *died*." He shook his head at his old friend. It had been a long time and he had imagined Basil coming back, but not like this.

"I apologized for that!" Basil wasn't listening and now Tom was growing frustrated.

"When? Ten years later? You can't expect such a late apology—" His voice was stern, but Basil just interrupted him.

"You *know* it was an accident… Why didn't you defend me?" Basil stepped closer to Tom. The man didn't look much different than ten years ago and he deeply regretted having left. He felt the urge to reach out to him. He felt so lost and angry. Nothing was going the way he had planned. All this time and the first thing Tom does is remind him of his past faults. Basil seethed.

"Basil... I didn't know anything. You left after the first person died. You knew what had happened and you didn't do anything to fix it. All of the fisheries were shut down. We almost lost everything, and we had to bury so many... Nothing I could have said would have mattered."

Basil stared at the floor, his fists balled at his sides. He was at a loss for words. "I've trained so hard... I'm so much stronger now. I know so much more." He looked up at Tom desperately. "I won't make that same mistake again."

"It's not me you have to convince, Bas... The families of those people are still mourning the loss of their children, their elders. How can you still be so arrogant?" Tom couldn't believe what he was hearing. Was Basil taking no responsibility?

"Then come with me, Tom." Basil took his friend's hand. "Let's go start our own town, somewhere else. We'll start with magic and people won't need to fear it anymore."

"I'm not leaving." Tom stood tall and firm. He jerked his hand back. "I love it here, and they need me. The lighthouse needs me as much as I need it." He gestured around himself.

Basil pushed Tom into the door, desperation in his eyes. He suddenly realized he hadn't learned anything, not where it mattered most. But it was too late. Magic had escaped his hands from his rage and into Tom's chest as he hit the door and the man crumpled at Basil's feet, the light fading from his eyes. Basil stared at his friend, shocked, and then stared at his own hands in horror. There was no blood; Tom's heart had just stopped. It had been so quick that there hadn't even been a look of pain on Tom's face, just surprise.

For a long moment that felt like an eternity, Basil stared at what he had done. He was in shock. When the panic finally set in, he did the only thing he could think of. He dragged Tom's body away from the door, placing him just so, and fled the house. Everything had happened so fast. He didn't know what to do, only that he needed to run away. He pulled a pole from out of his pack and extended it. Glancing back at the lighthouse, tears finally formed in his eyes. He mounted his broom and flew off the cliff, over the ocean.

How had he not learned anything in all this time? He thought he had learned so much, but it still hadn't been enough. He unwittingly killed the only person that mattered to him and was cast out from the only town he had considered a possible home. What was worse, he was running away. Again.

CHAPTER SIX

The grief had been excruciating. *Why did I do it? Why couldn't I control myself?* Ever since the accident, Basil hadn't done much of anything but sit on the floor of his room, ruminating over what had happened. What could he have changed, why had he gotten so angry? It was *their* fault. He wouldn't have gotten so upset if they had just listened. If they hadn't thrown rocks at him like some animal. And they must have put Tom against him, why else would he have denied him? It was infuriating! He held his head in his hands, fingers digging into his skin. He had been gone from Lightview for *ten years*. Wasn't that enough time to be forgiven?

Basil had been renting a room at The Schooner, an inn in Westdown, for the last few months since Tom's...unfortunate death. He hadn't known where else to go and hid his magic from the villagers here so as not to raise an alarm. He had heard whispers and rumors of his return to Lightview, and some claimed he had killed Tom, but the majority consensus was that he had died of heart failure. For now, he was in the clear. But it didn't make him feel any less guilty. He hated himself, but not as much as he hated the town that had created all of his misery in the first place.

He pulled himself to his feet, using the windowsill to help himself up. His legs had fallen asleep and he hit them with one balled fist as he felt the pins and needles spike through him. Grunting, he clumsily walked into the bathroom and ran himself a shower. He ran it hot; the scalding water turned his pale skin pink, but he didn't care how hot it got. For a time, he just leaned his forehead against the shower wall while the water ran over him. He felt nothing. He thought nothing. He was as empty as the bottle of hair wash on the shelf.

Somehow, he managed to dry himself off and safely reach his bed. As he sat down and stared at the cracks in the hardwood floor, something in him snapped. The numbness slowly receded and was replaced with remorse. But it wasn't for the town; this feeling was solely for Tom. He couldn't manage any more tears, but this feeling was enough to give him an idea of what to do next.

He got dressed and managed to eat a slice of toast before heading out with his bag. Behind the inn in the shade of an alley, he placed his palm over his chest and performed a few choice movements. He cast a spell of camouflage, becoming invisible to the townsfolk. He mounted his broom and flew off back to Lightview with a look of determination on his face.

Hair tied back, his bangs still flew up from the wind. But he could see. He knew now he shouldn't have left the town to begin with, but it was much, much too late to come to that realization. Lightview still looked the same. Nothing would change much after such a short time, anyway, though maybe he expected to still see grief on the villagers' faces.

Despite death, life continued on. They seemed content enough as he flew through the town, merely a breeze to the unknowing people around him. There were many faces he didn't recognize anymore after ten years, but that was hardly surprising. Even though he'd spent a year there, he hadn't made that many connections, though everyone seemed to know who he was. He had always been more focused on his studies than on other people. Tom had really been the only person he had wanted to spend time with. Now he had ruined that, too.

He headed first to the cemetery. Moss hung from the trees, looking ghostly with the fog that sat in a thick layer over the earth. He searched among the graves, first checking all the fresh flowers and mounds. There weren't many, and none of them were Thomas Hanna. Disgruntled, and only a little surprised that his grave wasn't here, he flew on his broomstick-pole back through the streets and towards the lighthouse. Tom had loved the lighthouse so dearly, he must have desired to be buried there.

Basil passed one of the many stores and saw a broomstick against its display window. This caught him by surprise and he couldn't help but stop to inspect it. Looking inside the store through the window, two young people carried boxes to a shelf and stocked them. He didn't recognize them and nothing looked out of the ordinary... He glanced back at the broom and realized it was just for cleaning, not a witch's broom at all.

As if they'd let a witch back in after me, he thought. *"We don't need witches here,"* they had said. Well, here Basil was again. He wasn't here to regain their trust anymore, though. He was here to make what amends he could with his dead friend.

He landed among the wildflowers at the lighthouse hill. The breeze brought the smell of the ocean and lavender. It was all too familiar and made his chest hurt. The idea that he had only been in this exact position that spring, banging on Tom's door... He stood there in the grass for a moment, his mind slowly emptying of torturous thoughts, and he almost dozed in the comfort of the nostalgia of his first visit there at Tom's lighthouse.

Basil blinked away his dissociation and stepped forward. Looking around, he didn't see anything like a grave or a marker. He walked around the entire building before he realized not only was there no grave, but the lights were on in the house. His mind suddenly reeled.

Is he not dead? Did I only think I killed him? He ran up the porch almost frantically to look in the window and saw...someone else. It was a young woman, a girl, maybe. She was sitting in front of the fire, reading. She had looked up briefly; she must have heard his footsteps, but when she didn't see anything, she went back to her book.

Basil slowly turned away from the window and leaned against the house with a soft *thud*.

Of course.

He had heard the rumors and he had felt Tom's heart stop. Everyone had been talking about it, whispering their condolences, but no one had really talked about a funeral. Where had he been buried? And who was this girl? Did she live here now?

He looked through the window again. There was a picture on the mantelpiece but he couldn't make the people out from where he was. As far as he could tell, everything in the room looked the same as it had when Tom still lived there.

The witch shook his hands for a moment to help get rid of his jitters, and then fixed his wind-blown hair. He took a deep breath and moved both hands from his chest down to his waist, undoing his invisibility spell. He didn't really feel any calmer, but he needed answers.

Basil knocked on the door.

Magnolia lifted her head for the second time. She thought she had heard someone walking up the porch steps earlier, but she didn't hear them again before the knock just now. She set her book down on the coffee table and got up to answer the door. Lifting aside the front door's curtain, she saw a man standing there, pale skin, dark hair... She didn't remember seeing him before, but for some reason he seemed familiar.

"Hi there... Can I help you?" The warmth from the fire escaped through the open door, but the brisk air felt nice on her skin. It was odd weather for the summer, but the ocean breeze always kept the lighthouse rather cool.

Basil chewed on the inside of his lip for a moment, suddenly losing his nerve. *You can't just stand there.* "Is...Tom around?" Despite already knowing the answer, he braced himself for her reply.

"You knew my uncle?"

Uncle? He nodded.

"I'm so sorry... But Uncle Thomas has passed." She hung onto the door frame as if it hurt her to say it as much as it hurt Basil to hear it. Basil was silent for a moment, listening to the wind blow as it brought clouds over the village. It had been a dreary day already and this wasn't improving anything. Maggie searched for the man's eyes behind his hair as he stood silent before her. She almost reached out when he spoke.

"I see." His voice was so quiet it almost sounded like a whisper. "You're his niece?" He looked at her as he spoke up and she nodded.

"What's your name? Were you a friend of Tom's?" She gave him another look-over, trying to place if she had ever seen him before but still failing.

Basil shook his head, ignoring her questions rather than answering them. The concern in her voice was palpable, but that didn't interest him. "Where was he buried?" Blunt and to the point. He just needed to find Tom's grave.

Maggie frowned and held the door close behind her. "In our home village in the mountains..."

"But *this* is his home," Basil burst out, stepping forward. Tom couldn't have had any other home but the lighthouse. He had loved it here.

"We carried out his will." Her eyes narrowed. Why was this man so pushy? Who was he to her uncle?

Basil was furious. It was a mistake. Tom would never have let himself be buried elsewhere. This was his home, and Basil needed to apologize to his dead friend. It was the only thing left for him to do. "Where is this village? I must go there at once."

Magnolia started to feel scared. His tone had become threatening, and his outburst hadn't helped. "It's not for you to know. Good day." She began to close the door on Basil.

But he stuck his foot in the doorway and pushed his hands against the door. Despite his thin frame he was still stronger than Maggie. "Don't you dare! Where is he buried?" he yelled.

Maggie shrank in fear from his voice but she held her ground and pushed against the door with all her might. "I wouldn't threaten a witch so openly," she cried. The fire in its hearth blazed and the wind howled outside, shaking the windows of the lighthouse home.

Basil was beside himself. At first, he did nothing. He had let go of the door, though Maggie still tried to slam it closed on his foot. *A witch, staying in Lightview?* He started to laugh. It startled the redhead, but he laughed all the more. Maggie pulled out her wand and slashed it at Basil, a strong gust of wind emitting from it to push him back. But Basil was ready; he swiped his hand down to stop the force. He had stopped laughing and his expression darkened.

"You think you can force me out?" he snarled, eyes narrowing to slits. He swiped his arm at the door, almost ripping it from its hinges with his magic, and it sent Maggie flying back with the force. He didn't need a wand to use magic, not since his new training without one. She cried out as she slid across the floor, hitting the trunk on the other end of the room.

The witch slowly walked into Maggie's home, staring at the girl with a blaze in his eyes. She tried to back away from him from the floor, but bumped her shoulders into the trunk again. She knew exactly who he was now, but what he had to do with her uncle was beyond her. The heat of the fire shrank in its hearth and the breeze outside seemed to calm.

Basil began to realize what he was doing and looked around himself suddenly. He was standing right where he had killed Tom. The image of his friend's lifeless body stained his mind and before Maggie could register what was happening, Basil turned around and quickly left her home.

Maggie sat on the floor, shaken and dumbfounded. She started to cry, her shoulders heaving with emotion. It began to rain outside, and while the small witch didn't want to, she forced herself to her feet and ran to the open door. She looked all around for the pale man's figure, but she was alone. The front door creaked and sat crookedly within its frame, so Maggie waved her wand to reconnect the hinge that had broken. She slowly closed the door, locked it, and sat on the floor, her knees pulled up to her chest.

The rain pattered against the roof as if in a sigh of relief. Locking the door wasn't much security against another, stronger witch, but it made her feel better just the same. She ran her hands over her face, fingers through her hair. She had only been sitting there a few minutes, but it felt like hours. Shakily, she got to her feet again and sat on the couch in front of the fire. It soothed her shaking limbs and she took a deep breath.

He has to have been Basil. There's no other witch that's been here, from what everyone's told me... What's he got to do with Uncle Tom? Maggie looked around her home as if seeing it for the first time. He had been so angry and sad, but that didn't excuse him for attacking her. She held her face in her hands.

What if he came back? What if he found out her uncle was buried in Emelle? Would he hurt her family? Was... Was Tom's death not an accident?

Maggie shook her head. No one would have wanted to hurt Tom. All he ever did was help people.

The rain continued to patter against the windows.

CHAPTER SEVEN

"That sounds terrifying." Canton put his hand on Maggie's shoulder. "Did he hurt you?"

Maggie rubbed her nose and shook her head. She felt ashamed for not having been able to really fight back or defend herself after Basil had attacked her. "I just hit my head when I fell...but it's nothing, I'm fine."

"That man is a menace and he should be cast out of this continent!" Old Nan stomped her cane on the floorboards of the shop. She didn't need it anymore, but she felt a bit empty-handed without it. In her unbridled fury, she raised it above her head, shaking it threateningly to no one in particular. "How dare he come back here. I bet he killed your poor uncle! There were whispers, you know." She pointed her cane at them.

"That's all they were, Ma. Whispers and rumors. He disappeared just like he did the first time." Jax handed Magnolia a bag of ice for her head. He was Bea and Canton's father. They looked a lot like him; dark brown hair, glasses and blue eyes like Canton. Bea had her mother's eyes, green as grass.

"Don't you defend him, Jax, he killed your father and he'd have killed us all if he'd stayed." Old Nan's nostrils flared.

"I don't... I'm sorry, I can't talk about this anymore." Maggie stood and headed to the door. It was still sprinkling out, but it was clearing now. Canton and Beatrice followed after her and Old Nan finally settled down.

"I'm sorry, dear," Old Nan said. She wrapped Maggie in her arms and patted her damp hair. "I know this is hard on you."

"The Guard's going to double when I tell the mayor. You should stay here until I get back." Jax put a hand on Maggie's shoulder and then left the shop, heading towards the mayor's home. Maggie turned to her friends and Old Nan and gave a small, but weak smile. "I'm sorry to put you out like this. I just didn't know what else to do."

"Don't be silly. You did the right thing in coming here." Canton gave a reassuring smile.

"Let's go upstairs and have some tea," Bea said. "You can relax in my room." She took Maggie's hand and led her up the steps to the apartment. Canton followed and Old Nan was left to watch the shop.

The Val's household was comfortable and bigger than Maggie expected. A piano stood in the living room along with a couch and a small television. Sometimes Maggie forgot about things like television, she didn't have one at her own home, but what she was really interested in was the radio in the corner. There were always interesting songs playing and it reminded her of her mother.

Down the hall was Beatrice's room. It was a little messy, with clothes and papers strewn about, but it definitely displayed Bea's personality. Pictures of marine animals were plastered on her walls, along with study notes, and her desk was a mess of material for her schooling.

"Sorry." Bea laughed nervously as she picked up some items to give Maggie a place to sit. She watched her brother consider sitting on the bed, and then he thought better of it and sat on the floor. He grinned at her; he knew she didn't like him sitting on her bed.

"Don't worry about it," Maggie assured her. She sat on the edge of Bea's bed and held the ice bag to her head. Her other hand just sat in her lap.

Just as they were getting settled, Alaina popped her head in. "Sorry, kids, but I heard you wanted some tea?"

"Thanks, Mom. I almost forgot." Bea got up to help her mother with the tray and passed the cups out. Maggie was grateful and sipped on hers eagerly. It wasn't a potion, but it was delicious and relaxing just the same.

"Thank you," Maggie said.

"Of course, dear." Alaina smiled. The sound of a crying child pulled her head back out into the hallway to check. "Dany's upset about something again." She sighed and looked back at the trio. "Maggie dear, if you need anything, don't hesitate to ask. Bea can get it for you." She winked. Maggie actually laughed, Canton, too, and Bea just sighed with a smile.

When they were alone again, Canton put his cup down and spoke up. "Can I say something? About your uncle..."

Maggie lifted her eyes from her tea to look at Canton. She nodded. She was feeling much better than before now.

"You said you didn't know what Basil had to do with your uncle earlier." Canton looked over at Maggie. "We heard they were friends, before Basil poisoned the fishery. Nan had mentioned it a few times."

"They were friends?" Maggie put the ice pack down and sighed. "I had no idea... I guess that makes sense that he would come back looking for him. Maybe he only attacked me out of grief?"

"I doubt it, Mags." Bea leaned forward against the back of her desk chair. She was sitting on it backwards.

"I think it's possible," Canton replied. "But that doesn't make him any less dangerous. You said he was trying to find where Tom was buried, and he got upset when you refused to tell him." He shrugged, unsure, but contemplative. "What if he's a necromancer?"

Maggie gave a disgusted look, but it wasn't meant to be unkind. "Necromancers aren't real. No witch has been able to raise the dead. But, it is strange…" She shook her head. "I've already thought about it too much. Can we talk about something else?" The idea of her uncle being part of some repugnant necromancy ritual was making her sick, even if it wasn't possible. Keeping her thoughts elsewhere was much more appealing. Canton gave an apologetic look and Bea started to excitedly show Maggie some of her field notes.

~*~

It had been two weeks since Basil had come and attacked Maggie at the lighthouse. She hadn't seen him since and she was grateful for that, but she still felt on edge from time to time, checking out her window to be sure the dark haired witch wasn't about to come crashing into her house.

She was glad to be home again, though, and just like Mr. Val had said, the Guard had doubled. They had come from Westdown and they would periodically trade out watches between the town and the lighthouse. It was a little unsettling, even if it was supposed to help her feel secure. They didn't have anything like the Guard in Emelle.

Since last week, Maggie had been helping Mikel's family to prepare for the Harvest Festival. Their son had come back to visit from the college in the west, and she was glad to see Mikel and Prairie so happy to be with him again.

Maggie hung up flowers and fabric flags along their market stand and even helped make fruit wine at the Williams' farm while her friends helped push down corn stalks for the maze. Things were starting to look sharp and Maggie had been informed that the ships were coming in soon with the fireworks. She hadn't ever seen any before, but they sounded really fun.

"I've heard they can set a forest on fire," Maggie said.

"We live in the mountains, so it's too dangerous to light there... Anyway, it would draw too much attention to our village. You would usually get invited there, rather than stumbling upon it or finding it on a map like Lightview or Westdown."

"Is it a secret, then?" Canton asked.

"Pretty much. My parents didn't really like to talk about it; they just said not everyone likes witches and kept it at that. But there were a lot of people there. Just not as many as there are here." She smiled.

Farmer Williams had a blade of grass between his lips and grinned at Maggie as he handed her a glass of fruit wine. "Here y'go, lady friend. A little wine is good for a hard day's work!" He offered some to Bea and Canton. Mikel came guffawing onto the porch, his straw hat bouncing on his head.

"That's some fine wine, Magnolia! This festival is gonna be a blast. Just a bit longer now. Will you come back to prepare more?"

Maggie sipped the wine and grinned at its sweet flavor. "Sure! I'll have to make something of my own, too."

"More potions?" Bea suggested.

"I think I'll try something a little different... We'll see," she said mysteriously.

"I wouldn't mind some more potions myself, girly." Old Pete had joined them and gave Maggie a wrinkled grin. He hadn't coughed a single time since she'd seen him again. "The old hip's good as new, thanks to you. Might be I can get young again with that magic of yours."

Maggie laughed. "I don't know about that, but I'm glad I could put a spring in your step, Pete."

"I'm sure we'll like whatever you bring to the table, Miss Witch." Old Pete winked at her.

Farmer Williams had given her a small bottle of wine to take with her and she saw her friends off back to their home before she flew back to her lighthouse.

Eager to get to work, Maggie lit the fire back in her

hearth and cracked open the window in the kitchen to let in a nice, light breeze. The overhead light was ample when she flicked it on, and was necessary for her experimenting. She had her bottles set out on the counter, and her ingredients and her mortar and pestle sat on the table. She tied the apron her mother gave her and took a moment to think about her, her fingers pressing over the embroidery with care. She'd be proud, Maggie was sure.

Back to the task at hand, she ground up flowers, berries, and twigs, and mixed them with water, some part fresh, some part salt water. She used her wand to cast a spell upon it and it exploded a pink cloud into her face, causing her to yell, spit and sputter.

"Dang," she muttered, wiping her face. She wondered where she had gone wrong.

Maggie spent hours in the kitchen trying different ingredients and spells. The kitchen was starting to look like multiple paint bombs had gone off, but she wasn't worried about the mess. She finally managed to cork a bottle and cheered in her seat at her success. She was so tired she was almost delirious, so she left everything where it was for now, and dragged herself to bed. She wrote down her method just before falling asleep, a satisfied smile on her face.

CHAPTER EIGHT

A storm had been sighted forming over the ocean off the coast of Westdown. Ships nearby had called over the emergency radio to alert the surrounding area of its current trajectory, which was now heading towards Lightview. The mayor alerted the town to stay calm and stay indoors, and that the storm would get worse before it would get better.

To be on the safe side, Maggie decided to close the shutters on all her windows upstairs. She closed the curtains, too, for good measure, and shut off whatever lights she wasn't using before heading downstairs. She noticed that the guard who was normally patrolling the outskirts of the peninsula was heading back into the village, and she hardly blamed him. No one wanted to be stuck outside in a rainstorm.

It was her first storm by the sea, but she knew her home was made for this kind of weather. The town, too. She was confident that if any damage was done, she could help take care of it with her magic. She decided the best course of action for now was to just hunker down and wait for the storm to pass.

There was a knock on her door and Maggie opened it to see Mikel. He had a large paper bag in his arms and a big grin. He wore a yellow raincoat and a knitted hat to keep warm, though the rain hadn't started yet.

"Hullo, Maggie. I brought some things over, just in case."

"Oh, you didn't have to do that, Mikel. I didn't expect you to come by!" She grinned, surprised at his unexpected arrival.

"I insist! Thought you might like a little somethin' to tide you over." Mikel lifted the bag a little higher to emphasize. She let him in and he followed her into the kitchen. He sat the bag on the counter for her, the paper crinkling noisily.

"There's some nice goodies in there. You've got a backup generator, and magic of course, but...you can't be too prepared!" He laughed.

"That's so kind of you, thank you." She peeked into the bag for a moment, impressed with how much he had fit in it.

"Yeah, well. You can't predict these things. But you'll be fine. Wind's pickin' up, so I better get back to the Missus. Stay safe!" And with that, he put his hood up and headed back into town.

"You, too!" She hollered to him as he made his way down the dirt path. "Stay safe..." She watched him disappear across the small bridge before heading back inside.

Thunder rolled in the distance and Maggie looked out of the kitchen window to see the clouds coming in. Everything was already pretty gray and she could see the wind picking up just like Mikel had said. The waves below crashed violently into the cliff, sending sea foam up past the edge every so often with a particularly swift breeze. She was glad to know that she was not that cliff, nor the sea foam.

Maggie peeked into the bag again, seeing dried meats and fruit, some cheese, another bottle of wine and some candles. She put the candles out on the counter and packed the food goods up into the cabinet above her head. It was really kind of Mikel to come all the way out here to bring her this, she thought. She'd need to thank him with a gift.

It was getting dark rather fast. Maggie was starting to wish that Mikel had stayed with her so she didn't feel so lonely, but she imagined Prairie wouldn't have liked being left alone herself. She chuckled a little at that and lit the hearth with her wand. The warmth from the fire always did something to keep her woes at bay, so that would have to do for now. That, and the picture of her family and Tom on her mantle staring back at her gave her a feeling of both happiness and homesickness. It would have been nice to have her uncle here now... She took a deep breath and rubbed her eyes, telling herself she was just tired. Best not think of that for now.

The crackling firewood competed to be heard over the howl of the wind that picked up outside, but that picture on the mantelpiece glowed in the firelight and that helped her smile return. It was the same picture that Tom had always kept there, from when she had been a young girl. It brought her a lot of happiness, and sadness, looking at it every once in a while.

She pulled the list out from her pocket that she had made for her new potions and mulled over it for a moment before setting it on the table. She would love to work on a new potion now, but she was too distracted by the oncoming storm. Better to not waste any ingredients for now.

Rain continued to patter against the windows and she watched as each drop kissed the glass and slid down to the sill. As the rain picked up, every individual drop connected to form a continuous, moving sheet of liquid.

Normally, Maggie enjoyed the rain, but it was the heavy winds that she wasn't familiar with. She decided a good distraction would be helpful, so she went over to the bookcase and picked up something light to read. Before she even sat down, though, she heard a strange sound echoing from the stairwell to the lighthouse.

Maggie looked up the stairwell with her mouth twisted slightly in confusion. The sound came and went and reverberated off the walls, making it sound as though the entire spire was vibrating. She went through the doorway to the stairs, took hold of the railing and cautiously made her way up the steps.

The guiding light still shone on defiantly through the rain and wind, but the witch could tell the storm was getting progressively worse. She almost made it to the top when what sounded like a cannon went off above her head, causing her to duck down on her current step and cover her head. Glass fell down the stairs and some bits caught in her hair and clothes, and she was left in darkness. The light had gone out. Her ears rang from the sound and she felt disoriented as she opened her eyes, trying to gather her bearings.

When it seemed like the glass had settled, Maggie looked up. She could see the wind blowing around the top and bits of glass slid down the steps. She lit her wand to help guide her, and stepped around the larger pieces of glass. When she managed to get to the top of the stairs, she saw that the windows around the light had broken in. She had to hold on tight to the railing to keep the wind from whipping her about; she couldn't believe how strong it was now! Her heart felt as if it was stuck in her throat, hammering away, and she felt the strain of her knuckles turning white against the railing as she gripped it.

Of course she was scared.

The windows shouldn't have broken; she didn't know much about how it worked, but she did know they were weather-proof. Maybe they just hadn't met a storm as strong as this? She didn't know what that implied, but she did know she could at least put the glass back together.

Though her hands were shaking, she planted her feet against the iron steps and let go of the railing as she concentrated her energy into her wand. She thought she heard something through the wind, but she didn't pay it any mind. It was only the wind, after all.

Raising both hands above her head, her lit wand shined brighter and each piece of glass picked itself up and floated back to the window panes against the wind. She felt the glass stuck in her hair tug and pull until it released itself and watched as they collected with the rest of the panes. When they had settled, there was a clicking sound, and the panes all sealed themselves to look as if they had never broken at all.

Maggie fell to one knee, exhausted, when she heard someone calling her name from the stairwell. The window panes still vibrated from the storm, but it was much less violent than before. She was sure they would stay together this time, or at least, she hoped so. Looking behind her, she turned and held onto the railing, leaning over to look down the stairs. Canton was rushing up the steps, soaking wet.

"Thank goodness, Maggie. You're alright." Canton was panting and took a moment to catch his breath. He stood just a few steps below her.

Maggie got to her feet and brushed herself off. She was lucky she hadn't gotten a cut from any of the glass but touched any exposed skin just in case. "Yeah," she exhaled. "Just a bit winded. Are you okay?" He looked just about as roughed up as she felt. It must have been his voice she thought she heard in the wind. She felt a little guilty about that, but he didn't appear to be hurt at all.

Canton seemed to have recovered and looked up at her with rain covered glasses. He took them off to try and dry them, but he was soaked so nothing he had on him helped. Maggie tried to hide a smile as she handed him a handkerchief from her pocket.

"I'm okay. Thank you." He took the cloth and used it to dry his glasses. "It sounded like a gunshot went off and then the light went out. Can you get it running again?"

"I haven't tried yet, I just got the windows fixed… What are you doing out in this storm? It's so dangerous out now," she chided him.

Canton laughed lightly. "It wasn't raining when I started out. I thought I'd make it, but it started pouring on the way over. I almost didn't even make it inside; the wind is insanely strong." He put his glasses, dry now, back on. "Bea wanted to check on you, but I made her stay home. I'm glad I did with that wind." He smiled encouragingly. "What can I do to help?"

Maggie rubbed the back of her neck and looked back at the light. "Do you know anything about lights? I sure don't." She laughed nervously and then shook her head, as if deciding something for herself. "No, I'll try something. Just hold on."

Canton looked on with some anxiety. He knew how important the light was for the village, but he knew Magnolia hadn't forgotten. She opened the door to the light and looked it over briefly. She couldn't see any wires missing, and there wasn't any water damage. Honestly, how the light went off at all despite the generator, and that all the other power in the house was still on... It was suspicious to Maggie, but she could see the lights of the boats off in the distance and she didn't have time to think about it anymore.

She felt her confidence rise. With her wand, she drew runes as if on an invisible wall and felt her hair practically standing on end as she focused her energy into the light. Carefully holding her wand out, arm outstretched, she kept that pose until her strength gave out. She gasped and fell forward, but Canton caught her before she took a tumble.

The light still wasn't on.

"What happened?" he asked gently.

"I don't know, I just need to try again," she said, panting. He helped her down to sit while she caught her breath. She could feel the sweat forming on her face but she ignored it. She wasn't used to this kind of magic, it wasn't the same as fixing glass or making a potion. It took more energy than she was used to and she worried she wouldn't have enough to do it a second time.

"Maggie, I don't mean to rush you, but those ships can't see the cliffs without the light, and with those waves...there's no telling where they'll drift." Canton had his hand on her shoulder in reassurance, but he was staring out the windows to the ocean below.

"I know, I know..." Maggie's voice was quiet and strained. She held her wand but kept it in her lap. She concentrated, trying to build up her energy again and focus her intention. With her mind focusing on the lamp, she imagined the inner workings. The electricity flowing through the wires, the gears that turned the bulb. Although she was mostly making it up, it was still integral to the process. Her toes tingled and she felt warmth just beneath her skin, slow and sweet like honey. The energy was there, then; she felt it rising. Her eyes were shut tight until the moment came when she opened them, feeling her energy at its peak.

She lifted her wand as if she was drawing a sword from its sheath and pointed it at the light with determination. For a moment, nothing happened. She almost started to cry in frustration as she pushed herself, leaning forward now on one arm as she couldn't bring herself to stand. But she kept at it, her heart full. Suddenly, there was a click and the light practically blinded her as it came back on, shining with its renewed intention to warn the oncoming ships at sea.

Maggie laughed out loud in elation and heard Canton behind her whooping with her in success. He hugged her tight and helped her to her feet. She laughed all the more at how wet he still was and managed a small drying spell to help him out.

"That was amazing, Maggie, look at how much magic you have in you," he exclaimed, holding her gently by the arms as she steadied herself with the railing.

Maggie still laughed and wiped the hair from her face. "I wasn't sure I had enough, honestly. But thank you." She brushed her hair from her eyes and took a deep breath, exhaling in relief.

Canton helped her down the stairwell and sat her down on the couch where she collapsed in the comfort of the cushions.

"I need you to bring me the potion inside the fridge," Maggie asked. She was feeling better now, but she was still weak. A wave of wind billowed against the house and rattled the nearby window, causing her to jump in alarm, but she didn't bother to look out. Her body felt too stressed to worry her mind any more with the storm. Canton came back quickly with the bottle she had asked for and she uncorked and downed it in one go.

The relief was quick. Her energy wasn't one-hundred percent, but she felt much better. She stretched her arms and legs out, closed her eyes tight and laughed. Canton smiled at her reaction. There was a flash from the window behind Maggie and a boom so loud it shook the earth. It sounded like splitting wood and thunder. Maggie turned around to see the tree just outside catch on fire: lightning had struck it. It was so close to the porch, she was afraid it would light the house next.

Maggie jumped to her feet and rushed out the door. Canton reached out to stop her; he was worried she'd get hurt by the buffeting winds or debris, but she was too fast for him. She jumped off the steps of the porch and out into the rain, water splashing as she landed in a puddle. The wind pushed against her but she fought her way to the flaming tree. She spread her wand out in an arc, her magic gathering the rain that fell into one large bubble, and she used it to douse the tree. This spell wasn't nearly as difficult for her as fixing the lamp, and she grinned to herself in satisfaction. The poor tree was looking worse for wear and was still being buffeted strongly by the wind, but at least it wasn't on fire anymore.

Another gust of wind came as Maggie turned to go back indoors and it pushed the witch right over. She put out her arms to catch her in her fall and landed roughly on her hands, then elbows. She grunted in pain, though it could have been worse.

"Where is he?" The voice was low but it had a bite of venom to it. It still carried through the wind, as cruel as the waves crashing against the cliffside. She knew who it was instantly.

Maggie pushed herself up to look behind her and saw

Basil floating down to the grass. The storm whipped around him, but he was untouched entirely. She realized then that he must have been the cause of the storm. Whether he had manipulated the one they had been warned about or started it entirely, Maggie couldn't imagine. That kind of spell was too strong, how could he possibly have that kind of power? And with no wand to help channel it? The same fear from before suddenly gripped her and she couldn't get herself to do anything but continue to sit there, staring at the older witch across the yard, even as Canton slammed open the front door and yelled something she couldn't hear at them.

"W-why does it matter where he is?" she stammered, pushing her wet hair from her eyes. "He's dead, just leave him in peace!"

"*I* killed him. I have to say goodbye!" With a movement Maggie couldn't see, a wave of wind from Basil pushed her away several feet and all she managed to do was raise her arms to shield herself in a last ditch effort of protection. Canton had been blown back inside the house.

Maggie was shocked, both by Basil's power and by his confession. This man was insane! The fear she felt seemed to evaporate, but instead of revitalizing her, it gave way to anger. She fought to get to her feet but her legs had turned to jelly. She just couldn't bring herself to stand. She started crying and she didn't care; they were tears of outrage and frustration.

"Why?" she yelled. "You were friends!"

Basil's expression seemed to boil over with rage. He whipped a wave of wind at her again, but this time it was stronger. Maggie raised her arms to shield herself again, but the wind was so sharp this time it cut her arm as it pushed her back. She cried out in alarm only to stifle herself and glare with fury at her adversary.

"I killed the others. Why not him? It was *their* fault. They put him against me!" He walked steadily towards her now, his hands raised in a shrugging gesture and then pointing at her as if it was her fault, too. He wasn't making any sense. He killed her uncle? Why was he doing this?

She struggled to her feet, her heart pumping in her ears, and drew her wand. The reason wasn't really important right now. He had to be stopped.

CHAPTER NINE

The power in her legs finally returned, and in a rage she'd never felt before she rushed forward at Basil, her wand aimed right at his face. He swatted her away easily with his magic, sending her sprawling. In her fall, she sent a pressurized shot of air at him, hitting him in the side of the head before he had time to react. The wind seemed to die down in his shock.

As she hit the ground, she pulled up mud and grass and had to wipe the filth from her face to see through the rain. Basil raised his hands to retaliate and Maggie pushed herself to her knees and cast a protection spell around herself just as lightning came down to strike her. She couldn't believe he could control the lightning, too. The pressure of it striking her magic shield knocked her back and her spell dissipated.

The rain kept up, but the wind was sporadic. Basil was just as soaked as she was now. She wondered if he controlled the storm at all anymore. He attacked her, his wand like a sword, and she blocked with her shielding spell, smaller than before and lowering it to parry. He cut her cheek and she cut his in return, and then she was in the grass again, her hair plastered to her face and her chest heaving in her exhaustion.

"Why are you doing this?" she screamed. She swiped her wand at him and it knocked him from his feet. *Finally!* Her muscles were weak with fatigue and her head felt fuzzy, but she stood back up anyway and stepped towards him. She could see he was still breathing, and she wasn't sure how she felt about that. This entire fight confused her, and even more so when she saw that Basil was crying. It would have been difficult to tell if it weren't for the red around his eyes, with the rain. She started to speak when he jerked forward and she blocked him with her shielding spell again. Just in time.

But it had been enough to distract her, and he was up in the air and flying away from her, back towards the town. Maggie *tsked* and ran back to her house. That he was so powerful he could fly away without a broom… She wished she was stronger, but she had no time for regrets now.

Stepping inside her home, the warmth of the fire made Maggie want to just crawl into bed and forget about all of this, but Canton was getting to his feet and holding his head as if in pain. "Oh my goodness, Canton, are you okay?" She had almost forgotten about him.

"I'm fine." He shook his head and wiped his hair from his eyes. "What about you? I saw you out there." He handed her the handkerchief she had given him when they had been in the stairwell and she used it on her face, wiping the mud and blood away. It was just a shallow cut on her cheek and a busted lip. She was glad to see Canton didn't have more than a small bruise from his fall, but she hoped he wasn't concussed.

"It's just a few cuts." She glanced at her arm, which was still bleeding lightly, and stepped across the room. Under the bathroom sink was a medical kit. She grabbed it and brought it back out into the living area. Inside were a few potions and she poured one onto her arm, causing the area to turn blue around her wound. She started to wrap it in gauze to help it heal properly, but fumbled with the material.

Canton was standing by, feeling somewhat useless until Maggie dropped the gauze. He quickly reached down to pick it up and deftly finished wrapping it around her arm. He smiled at her, feeling suddenly shy, as he tucked the last piece in.

"Thank you," Maggie said. Thankfully, it didn't sting; merely tingled. Canton shrugged in response.

"Where did Basil go?" he asked, fiddling his hands together.

"Back into the village. I have to go." Canton's surprise wasn't lost on Maggie, but she summoned her broom with her wand anyway. "He says he killed Tom. I think he's blaming the villagers... He started the storm and I think he's going to try and kill someone. No one here can stop him but me." Despite her brave words, she was shaking. She wasn't made for fighting. The spells she used weren't meant to kill anyone, and as far as she knew, they probably couldn't.

Basil, on the other hand, had apparently killed her uncle and several villagers. She had no idea what kind of skill set he had, but from his storm and their battle, it wasn't something she felt confident she could stand up against. It was way too advanced.

But there wasn't anyone else. Her broom floated beside her obediently and she pulled her hair up into a bun to keep it out of her face. A coat hung beside the front door, as well as her black hat, and she donned both. She moved her wand down her body to dry and clean herself from the rain and mud she was covered in, and then cast a spell on her clothes to keep her as dry as she was able before mounting her broom. The fireplace crackled. It was a merry sound, much unlike their current situation. Warm and inviting, and lulling Maggie to stay where it was much safer than out there. She swung open the front door.

"See ya'." And she was gone.

Canton didn't have time to say anything and he ran his hands through his hair as he watched her go. He hated not being able to do anything. Like she'd said, this was beyond anything anyone at the village could handle. He wished his sister was with him now. She always had a way of cheering him up, even at the worst of times. All he could do was stare out the window and warm himself by the fire, hoping that Maggie would come back safely.

Despite the lull in the storm, the tide was still incredibly high. Maggie flew over the flooded bridgeway and worried briefly of Canton trying to leave the lighthouse. The rain would have impeded her vision if not for her spells; the brim of her hat kept the rain from her face and her coat was keeping her warm for now. But her stomach was in knots. All the energy she had expelled in their fight had made her famished, and she was anxious and worried besides. Her hands gripped her broom so tightly she briefly wondered if she'd snap the wood in half.

Try to relax. Calm as a summer breeze. Maggie took a deep breath as she flew over the village, looking around for Basil or any evidence he'd been there. All she could hear was the pounding of the rain against her hat and coat, and she couldn't see much, either. No one would be out in this weather; they'd all been told to stay inside.

~*~

He hadn't sustained any serious injuries, but he was exhausted and furious. What did that witch girl know about Tom? Niece or not, Tom had never mentioned her. She didn't know *anything*. He would show her... He'd show her exactly why witches weren't welcome in Lightview. If they were all going to be against him, he'd give them a real reason to be.

Tom was dead, nothing could bring him back, and as far as he was concerned, the town had put Tom against him. They had poisoned his mind with their lies and their fears. It was their fault he was dead. *If I had just been given a chance to redeem myself...* But it was too late for that.

The girl was stronger than he had thought. He didn't even know her name, but there was something about her. Still, she was nothing compared to him. He let the rain come, cleansing

87

him as he landed in the streets of Lightview. No one seemed to be out in this awful weather, but that didn't concern him any. He would make them come out. He didn't have anything left to lose.

The witch flicked his wand at a nearby building, sending waves of wind into it. They crashed into the roof, sending wood and tiles flying. Someone screamed as their roof was destroyed, and he briefly saw them through the rain in the new window he'd opened. He laughed and didn't bother to wait for anyone to come out before moving on to the next building, sending out more magic until he reached the courtyard where the mayor's home sat nestled beside the clock tower. Instead of wind, he sent a ball of fire, lighting the front door.

"Stop!"

Basil turned, expecting the little witch to be there. But it was some other girl, a villager, it seemed. A dark look came over his face.

Beatrice stood, her feet planted in the cobblestone and her fists tightened at her sides, and stared Basil in the face. She was drenched and she was cold, but one of Basil's attacks had hit her house and before her father could stop her from running out into the storm, she had slid down the stairwell and was out the door, following Basil's retreating form. She saw him attack several other houses, but it was when he started to use fire that she finally found the nerve to confront him and not just follow after him. She could hear the door crackling in the flames and she hoped the mayor wasn't asleep.

Before she could blink, a pillar of stone came up behind her. Something seemed to reach out and trap her arms behind the stone. It lifted her off her feet and she cried out in pain at the weight it put on her shoulders and arms. She couldn't tell what her hands were bound in, but she could barely move her fingers and her eyes felt hot with tears. She hadn't even seen him move.

Basil had grown the trap from the earth and cobblestone beneath Bea's feet. He stalked towards her, his hair smeared against his face, his wand gripped tight in his hand.

How insolent; she wasn't even looking at him. He raised his wand when a smoking shot of green hurled into the cobblestone at his feet. He jumped back and covered his face, unsure if the smoke itself was toxic.

Maggie jumped off her broom and slashed another ball of fluorescent green at Basil. He summoned the ground up to form a wall, blocking the gelatinous substance. It dripped and oozed down the cobblestone and smoked as if it was acid, but the stone was unharmed. Basil rolled out from behind his shield and shot fire, and Maggie blocked with her summoned shield. Part of her sleeve still managed to catch fire and she patted it out hastily. For the flames to catch the fabric in this rain *and* get through her shield, it must have been a highly advanced fire spell. She fought against a feeling of dread.

The ground around her started to sink and she almost lost her footing. Maggie shot another green glob at Basil and it hit him in the gut, disrupting his spell, and the ooze traveled down to his feet and locked him in place. Before he could react again, she knocked the wand from his hand with a gust of wind. She stepped over the malformed stones and ran up to Beatrice, her hands on the girl's hips so as to reassure her. She couldn't quite reach her shoulders with how she was lifted.

"Oh, Bea." Maggie had tears in her eyes for her friend. She could tell how strong Beatrice was being, but the girl couldn't bring herself to speak. Maggie went around to the back of the pillar and saw that Bea's wrists were encased in a cobblestone set of cuffs connected to the pillar. She shot a disgusted look at Basil, furious that he would do this to her friend and for no reason, but even in her anger she couldn't bring herself to say anything. She tapped her wand on the binding and the stone crumbled around Beatrice's wrists, causing her to fall to the ground.

Basil was yelling obscenities and curses, but nothing happened from them but a weak gust around his form. It was just noise. He had used magic without a wand before. Maybe he'd finally run out of energy. Her hope was that the goo she'd encased him with would prevent him from any subtle hand movements. Maggie ignored him while she helped Bea collect herself against the pillar. "Are you okay?" she whispered to her friend. Bea nodded and held her arms against herself.

The door to the mayor's house crashed outside his home, the flames faltering in the rain after it had eaten through the wood around the hinges. The mayor scrambled around inside the house, putting out the fire that had spread and caught on his curtains.

The storm picked up again and lightning flashed overhead. Whether it was Basil's doing, or the storm had picked up on its own, Maggie couldn't tell. She stepped in front of the witch, her hands balled into fists, and she suddenly slapped him. The goo she had cast on him had encased his arms at this point, but it wasn't traveling any farther up. There were onlookers from all the windows in the courtyard, but they kept their distance.

"Why did you do all this?" Her tone was exasperated and sad.

Basil had run out of steam and hung his head in his prison. The ooze had hardened. It took him a moment to speak, but finally the words came. "I wanted to say goodbye." His voice was cracked and hardly audible.

She almost expected his response. "Tom wouldn't have wanted this." Did he know her uncle at all? She narrowed her eyes, but she still felt a cloud of grief about her.

"He wouldn't have wanted me to kill him, either." The witch looked up at the redhead. He looked pathetic. Wet hair covered half his face, a look of defeat cut deep in his eyes. He had been manic, he knew, but controlling himself had been out of the question. Now he was just dead tired. He hadn't been able to work up the energy to cast a spell without his wand. It seemed the right time to give up.

"We were told it was a heart attack..." Maybe he was just reacting badly to his friend's death? The idea that he just imagined it all was better than the alternative, she felt.

"It was an accident," he admitted. His head hung again. "I ran away when my experiment failed. An old man died suddenly, after he'd eaten the fish. I knew they'd blame me...but I couldn't handle it. So I left." He tried to stretch his arm to his face, but it wouldn't budge. He sighed in exasperation.

"I was gone too long. I snuck back into town, just to see...and more people had died. Everyone blamed me. I was just trying to improve their lives. But I wouldn't have been able to save anyone anyway..."

Maggie wanted to slap him again, but instead she stomped her foot and spoke up. "That's not true! You could have stopped anyone else from eating it. You could have found a way to cure them." She couldn't believe how lost he was. It was almost heartbreaking, but she was too angry to sympathize.

"When I finally did come back, everyone still hated me," he said angrily. "They wouldn't let me stay, even though I could help them *now*. And when I went to Tom, he was against me, too. I didn't mean to hurt him...but I was so angry."

Maggie could hear the remorse in his voice, but she was still confused and upset. She couldn't find it in her to forgive him, or to even understand him. He was like a petulant child, blaming others for his mistakes and running from his problems.

The villagers were coming out of their homes now as the rain seemed to let up again and she could hear their murmurs. They turned to shouts and she turned back to look at them. Accusing fingers pointed at Basil from all around, matching their anger. He started to struggle against his bonds, wishing to get away from all this.

"You're the reason our Thomas is dead?"

"How dare you!"

"You came back to kill us, just like we thought."

Maggie spoke over the villagers to Basil, "It's not right to hurt someone just because you don't agree with them." Their voices seemed to bring her back to the reality she was facing and she frowned all the more.

Basil shook his head. "I know, I...lost control." He whispered, "I'm weak."

"We should kill him, look. He's trapped." The crowd was getting rowdy again.

"That's not what we do here. Listen to Magnolia." Mikel stepped out from the crowd and stood behind Maggie, a tall and commanding presence. He crossed his arms and stared his fellow villagers down. "We're not a mob out for blood. Let them work it out." This seemed to quell the voices, but the atmosphere was still tense. They had started to trust Maggie, but Basil was a man they just didn't understand. He had powers that scared them, and a past some of them still remembered very well.

"The magic just...poured out of me," Basil said. "I learned new techniques where I didn't need to use a wand." He didn't like admitting it, but it was the first time he could finally talk about how Thomas died.

"But you're too emotional and it ended up controlling you," she finished for him. Maggie rubbed her face in frustration. "What are we going to do with you?" she muttered. "What is it you want? I can't trust you, you know... Not like this."

Basil couldn't bring himself to look at the villagers. He appeared to be turning inward all the more, and his voice was getting quieter all the while. She was afraid of him, but she was starting to understand why he ended up like this. Grief and anger had taken over without much resistance, clouding his judgment. But he was regretting his mistakes. "I don't know," he said, finally.

"You do," she replied. "Don't you want to apologize?"

"I…" He shook his head. He knew it hadn't been a true apology when he had come back to the village. Tom had been right. "Please, release me and I'll apologize properly."

A feeling of panic filled the courtyard, but Maggie lifted her wand immediately despite all that. A part of her believed he wouldn't try anything to harm them. The ooze softened and disintegrated into green mist and Basil fell to his knees. Immediately, he lowered his head to the ground, hitting his forehead on the cobblestone roughly. Maggie winced at the sound. He seemed to have done it purposefully.

"I'm so sorry," he said, his voice rough but audible. "My magic went awry, and I unintentionally killed your loved ones." He squeezed his eyes shut tight, as if that would transport him somewhere else than where he was. To apologize made his guts feel like jelly and he wished, for all his magic, that he could just disappear. "I know an apology isn't good enough. Nothing I can do will bring them back. I was a fool." He hit his forehead on the cobblestone again. "I still am." The emotion cut through his voice again.

The mayor, his curtains and door no longer on fire, slowly made his way through the crowd and to Maggie's side. He stared down at the witch on the ground and wiggled his mustache in thought. "While unintentional, murder cannot go unpunished. This is a very serious offense." He looked at Maggie and thought for another moment. "Basil. We have no reason to welcome you back here. But you did a wonderful job improving our lives until that disaster with the fisheries. We don't want that to be repeated. You don't seem a very stable man, Basil…and if it weren't for Magnolia here, I'm not sure we'd even be having this conversation. That is a frightening thought." He patted Magnolia on the shoulder. "Miss Hanna, thank you very much for subduing this villain. He killed your uncle. What say you?"

Maggie reeled. "Are you asking me to choose his fate?"

The mayor's brow narrowed in a sort of serious confusion. "We are talking murder, Magnolia, and you'd know best, I think."

Maggie pushed her hat back and it hung from a loop around her neck. Sweat had soaked the hair across her forehead and she pushed it away, grateful for the cool air that replaced it. Basil was still hunched over, his head against the cold, wet cobblestone, and she stared down at him cooly while considering her options. He seemed as still as a rock, but she could just barely see him shaking. There really wasn't any other choice.

"We can't kill him," she said suddenly. The mayor merely clicked his tongue, but the villagers muttered amongst themselves, uncertainty laden in their voices.

"Then you will watch over him," said the mayor. "He'll finish the job he failed to complete before he left and fix the mess he's made here. He will serve us for the next five years."

Maggie hadn't had much interaction with the mayor. She had been welcomed to town and they'd had a few meetings, checking on her progress and how she was getting along with the villagers—not that anything seemed to change from those meetings—so she was shocked at his deadpan tone and sudden decision. She turned her head slowly to look back at Basil, who still hadn't moved from his spot on the ground.

"What's to stop him from escaping?" she asked, disbelieving.

"You. You're the only other person here that can use magic. Who else could keep him in line?"

It felt like a punishment. But he was right, there wasn't anyone else and there wasn't any time to teach a town afraid of magic any useful skills to help them do it themselves. She wondered how her uncle would have really felt, if he had known from the beginning that Basil had acted by mistake...and that Maggie had the power to give or take the life of his killer.

94

Were Basil and Tom as close as all that? Would he be proud of her for her choice? Even with Maggie's presence, Basil could just disappear at any point. She couldn't possibly keep him in line if he wanted to leave.

This all felt like too much. Her entire being felt like lead and her vision became blurry. All she did was close her eyes, and she fell backwards. Her knees had buckled beneath her.

Surprised, Mikel shouted before he caught her. He lowered her to the ground carefully as Bea hurried to her side. Her wrists were bandaged and still throbbing, but it didn't stop her from worrying about Maggie. Quiet, concerned questions escaped her, but Maggie couldn't quite understand what Beatrice was saying. She fell unconscious, silence and darkness the last thing she remembered.

CHAPTER TEN

When Maggie woke up it was in her own bed—Tom's bed—and the realization filled her with relief. She had grown used to his bed by now, and it even gave her comfort, where before it had only caused her grief. A warm, cloudless sunlight shone through her open window and she could smell the sea on the breeze. She had half expected to be somewhere else, like back in the courtyard in town, and the fact that she wasn't made her feel as though her memories of yesterday were all just a bad dream.

"Mornin', darlin'," said a kind, recognizable voice from a robust woman. Prairie leaned forward from her chair beside Maggie's bed to pull the cloth from the witch's forehead. "You've been out a whole two days."

"Two days?" Maggie repeated, looking back out the window. Her stomach growled and she groaned in response. So much for only 'yesterday'. "Basil—"

"He's downstairs, honey. Makin' breakfast. The townsfolk won't let him fix a thing until you get your rest back. We were all pretty darn worried about you, y'know." She smiled warmly at Magnolia and the witch felt like another sun was shining down on her.

So it was all real, and the aches and pains she felt weren't from some illness but from their fight. She let out a long sigh and closed her eyes. "Are Canton and Bea okay? Where's Mikel?"

Prairie looked Maggie up and down, as though checking to make sure she was well enough for a conversation. She exhaled with a small, knowing smile. "They'll be fine," she said. "Bea was a little shook up, bless her, but she's recovered fast. She's downstairs with Basil, making sure that fool doesn't poison your food. Not that I see any cause for worry at this point, but I understand her concern. Still, that man's been so quiet and forlorn he'd probably forget to feed himself if those two weren't watching him like a hawk." She squeezed Maggie's hand in reassurance. "Mikel, now, he's been running the shop while I've been here with you. Thankfully, the festival's only been postponed and not cancelled altogether. We'll get it all sorted out soon."

Magnolia found a small smile inside her and felt another wave of relief, despite the confusing circumstances with Basil. With Prairie and the Val siblings there with her, the male witch didn't seem as frightening. She finally sat up in bed and rubbed the sleep from her eyes. Her body didn't ache as much as she thought it would, now that she was up. She felt the cut on her cheek, scabbed over, and turned to the door when she heard someone coming up the steps.

Basil stood in the doorway with a platter of food, that forlorn expression on his face that Prairie had warned her of. Beatrice was right behind him, her brow furrowed and a look of impatience plainly displayed. When she saw that Maggie was up, her expression changed immediately and she practically pushed Basil aside as she squeezed around him to greet her.

"You're finally awake!" Prairie got up from her seat and Beatrice sat in her place, taking Maggie's hands in hers. "I wondered why he was making you solid food. He suspected you'd wake today." She didn't like giving him praise and shot him a suspicious look. It seemed only half-sincere, though. At least, it seemed that way to Maggie. The redhead laughed quietly.

"I didn't realize I was gone for so long. But it's good to be up again."

Basil sat the tray in her lap abruptly, the cutlery clinking against the plateware. Although she was a little shocked at the sudden action, the food looked delicious and was still steaming with heat. Eggs, toast with jam, bacon and fresh berries all looked up at her, tempting, and she found herself salivating already.

She didn't wait to eat. She was close to tipping the glass of juice over in her haste and Bea took it from the platter quickly, laughing as she did.

"Wow." Bea grinned. "Two days out can do that, I guess." She glanced behind her at Basil, who stood against the far wall watching them. He was fiddling his fingers together and feeling as awkward as he appeared. When Maggie started to slow down, Beatrice handed her juice back.

"Thank you," Maggie managed to say between bites as she glanced over at Basil. She downed the juice and finally finished her plate, pushing the tray away. The three others in the room were silent, each surprised in their own way at her thanking him. Maggie was wiping her mouth with a napkin when she looked up to see Basil staring at the floor. "It was good food, and it didn't kill me, so…" She offered a sheepish smile.

"You don't need to keep bringing that up," Basil snapped, still staring at the floor.

Maggie frowned. "You need to let that go. I might not have been here then, but these people were, and they haven't killed you or thrown you out yet. So it looks like you need to come to terms with your mistakes instead of taking it out on others."

Prairie covered her mouth, stifling a laugh. It had been hard for her to accept Basil in Magnolia's home, cooking and cleaning for her… She had to whip him into shape whenever he made a backhanded comment or complained about a chore. But he was doing alright. That didn't mean she had to start liking him, though. Watching Maggie chastise him made up for all of the time she had to spend around him the last few days.

Basil rubbed his face roughly and then ran his fingers through his hair. He sighed. "You're right. I'm sorry." Dark eyes looked up to reach Maggie's. He was still acting like a child, but he seemed to be trying. Maggie sighed quietly but smiled regardless. This wasn't going to be easy.

"Bea, why don't you help me downstairs?" Prairie motioned Beatrice to follow her out, and Bea, about to protest, looked between Basil and Magnolia and grudgingly got to her feet, taking the tray with her.

When the door closed, Maggie offered a half smile to Basil, who was still glowering across the room. She held her arms for a moment in silence until she decided to offer him a seat at the empty chair beside her bed. "I think we need to talk."

Basil didn't move for a moment. His immediate reaction was to just leave. Maybe jump out the open window and fly across the cape again. But, no. Wrinkling his nose to display his distaste, he slowly walked the few feet across the room and sat down in the wooden chair. He still smelled damp, like he hadn't changed his clothes since the storm. It wasn't entirely off-putting, but it wasn't exactly pleasant, either. Maggie couldn't help but frown. He wasn't taking care of himself, like Prairie had said.

"I know I've been a right ass." He found his voice before Maggie managed to speak. But then he lost it soon after, unable to find the proper words to express himself. His eyes were downcast to his hands in his lap.

Maggie folded her legs criss-cross and leaned against the ledge beneath the open window. A breeze lightly lifted her unbraided hair away from her neck. "Good," Maggie said outright. Basil looked at her, and then looked away. She thought she saw a small smile. She even smiled a little herself. She looked away from him as she spoke again.

"My name is Magnolia. I guess we never introduced ourselves." She smirked a little at that. "Tom was my uncle. It would have been easier...if his death hadn't been your fault." Her brow narrowed and she closed her eyes. It was still hard to talk about him, especially now. She stole a glance to see wet on Basil's cheeks. "But...it's not too late." She took a deep breath. That was hard to talk about, too. She didn't want to forgive him, and for now, she still hadn't. It hurt, and she wanted to scream. She wanted to cry. Maybe Basil had cried enough for her. She bit her lip before speaking again.

"Maybe one day I'll take you to where we buried him. But for now, we have to fix the things you've damaged. Are you agreeable?"

Basil wiped his face with his sleeve, nodded his head, and extended his hand out to her. She stared at it briefly before shaking it.

Well, she didn't die. And he felt warm. Maybe he wasn't so cold after all.

"I hate myself for what I've done," Basil admitted. "I don't think...I ever took the time to really listen to anyone around me. Even Tom. And I loved him." He shook his head. "I keep thinking it's too late...to save myself, or redeem the wrongs I've made." He rubbed his eyes wearily and leaned back in his chair. "It would have been easier if you had just killed me." His quiet laugh was hollow, and sad.

"It's never too late to change yourself, Basil. Being aware of what you've done and that you need to change is the first step." Each of the deaths at his hands weren't malicious or on purpose. But it was a huge toll, and Maggie wasn't sure what to say about that. "You're incredibly lucky," she found herself saying, "that you get to live. Maybe you can make the best of it this time."

Basil stared at the young woman, deep into her shining eyes. Even with her aches he knew she felt, the mussed hair, the scab on her cheek, the fatigue she was still coming out of: her personality shined through those eyes. It reminded him so much of Tom. He managed to smile, fighting back his tears. He was so tired of reacting rather than really seeing. He nodded, then, and leaned forward. Maggie almost pulled back, but stopped herself. He pulled out a small vial from his pocket, stuck his thumb in it and wiped it across Maggie's cheek, immediately healing the scab beneath it.

"I can teach you to heal with your saliva," he said, taking her bandaged arm. "But you seem pretty adept at potions."

"Is that one mine?" She let him remove the bandage and smiled when Basil gave a surprised sound. The cut on her arm had completely healed, leaving only a fading light blue mark along where her wound would have been.

"Well, yes." He inspected the vial and shook its contents lightly. "I found it in the bathroom earlier."

"Snooping?"

Basil couldn't help but smirk. He shrugged, almost playfully. "A little." He tossed the bandage into a wastebasket and got to his feet. "I guess...you should probably bathe. I'll draw the bath for you." He left the room and Maggie gathered the blankets up around herself, not sure how to feel, except a little mystified.

~*~

The bath was a much needed reprieve. Basil put salts in the water and she had put a small potion in, too. Her aches seemed to melt into the water and she felt revitalized. Afterwards, she dried her hair quickly with her wand and brushed it out manually, enjoying the simplicity and time it took as she sat on the porch. Canton had left to tend to his family's store, but Bea had her books with her and was sitting in the kitchen scribbling away into her notes. She still didn't want to leave Maggie alone with Basil, since Prairie had left as well.

Basil was in the yard, tending to the tree that had caught on fire during the storm. Maggie had never seen such quick revitalization magic before, and watched as the tree healed over and began to sprout new leaves and limbs right before her eyes. For Maggie, her magic seemed to need to settle in at least a day before she saw any changes to the plant. Despite her misgivings, she was impressed.

Maggie had found that there really wasn't anything for her to do in her home; Basil had cleaned the entire building from top to bottom while she was unconscious. She had even seen him washing the dishes by hand after she had woken up, and this surprised her the most.

"I would have balked at the idea of manual labor," he had told her. "But Tom always said it was the hard work, sweat and tears that would build this town. I think he meant it would build me, too."

Maggie smiled, thinking back on what Basil had told her now, but there were tears in her eyes. "He used to say the same thing to me." She looked at Basil from across the yard as he walked towards her. "About hard work… What you said earlier." Tom always told her she would be a great witch someday, too. She wondered if Tom ever said the same to Basil, or if he had loved Basil as much as he loved Tom. She had no idea her uncle had ever had such a relationship. He had never mentioned him during her visits, as few as they were, but then, he might not have met Basil when she had visited. Tom was still a pretty new arrival himself at that time, and Maggie had been very young.

"Magic is still better, though." Basil smirked. "Only peasants balk at magic, am I right?"

Maggie gave him a disdainful look.

"Don't you think you should rest some more now that you're awake before you go flying again?" Beatrice came out onto the porch and was worrying her hands together as she looked between Maggie and Basil. "I mean...to get your *strength* back. You know?" She smiled sheepishly, hopefully. The witch shook her head, smiling. She knew what Bea was implying, that she might not be strong enough to keep Basil in line, but even at full health she wasn't worth much salt if he really wanted to escape. She wouldn't say that to Bea, of course, not when her friend was as worried as she was.

"I've slept enough, my potions have already worked their magic, and your help and everyone else has lifted my spirits. I'll be fine, Bea." She crossed her arms and looked up at Basil. "I think Basil's about as raring to go as I am, so there's really no need for concern."

Surprising as it was, it was true, too. It was hard to see, but the hint of a smile sat on Basil's lips as he slung Maggie's bag over his shoulder. To Beatrice, though, it looked a bit creepy and unsettling. She stared at Maggie with a pouting lip, but said nothing.

"Why don't you ride in with us? It's a long walk back into town and you should probably see Canton and your parents," Maggie suggested.

Bea agreed and packed her things. Once they were all back outside, Bea mounted Maggie's broom behind her and Basil got on his pole broom. They rose up, that familiar feeling of wind invigorating Magnolia's spirit, and headed into town. Maggie could feel the end of summer on the breeze and thought of the fruit wine she'd made at the Williams' farm. She'd be glad for all this to be behind her, and to enjoy the festivities of the Harvest Festival.

When they arrived in the square, landing softly from their brooms, most of the villagers nearby kept their distance. Maggie just smiled despite how uneasy she felt. She wondered if they hated her for sparing Basil's life, but if they could just see how regretful he was, and willing to change, maybe they would respect her decision and be more open to magic.

A group of villagers came up to them suddenly and crowded around Magnolia. "Thank you so much," one woman said. "We know you did the right thing. We'll help however we can to get the village fixed up." The woman that spoke for them shook Maggie's hand, grinning like a child. The others with her looked just as pleased, though Maggie could see their eyes wandering over to Basil with disdainful looks.

Basil slipped away towards the mayor's home. His sullen look came back easily, but he didn't care who saw. Sliding Maggie's bag off his shoulder to rest on the ground, he took out his wand. He could feel the stares and heard the gasps. One woman muffled a yell under her hand from surprise, but one look at Maggie, calm as still water, and nothing more was to be done but to see what Basil did next.

He simply raised his wand like a conductor at a symphony and magicked the door, which was lying half destroyed on the cobblestone, back to its original state. It floated back to the door frame and reattached to the hinges, clicking into place. The mayor was watching from the window and gave a surprised twitch of his mustache as the door fixed itself. He opened the door and poked his head out to look at Basil and the crowd that had gathered.

"Good work, son," he said, adjusting his glasses. "I'll need you to fix these drapes and furniture, too." He opened the door wider to let Basil inside.

"How did you get him to change like that?" the woman from before asked Maggie.

Magnolia shrugged. "He's not evil... He finally realized the mistakes he made were his own fault and no one else's, and he wanted to do something about it." She rubbed her arm and glanced at Beatrice, feeling somewhat unsure. "I think he wants to make it up to my uncle, Tom."

"Hard chance, that. Killing him and all." The woman *tsked* and shook her head.

"They were all accidents," Maggie said, a little harshly.

The woman looked back at her, surprised at her tone. Maggie lowered her gaze and rubbed her brow. "If he does what he says...I think even my uncle would forgive him."

Bea put her hand on Maggie's shoulder in support. She knew it wasn't easy for her friend to speak of her uncle's death. Maggie was still struggling with accepting it, but it was slowly becoming more bearable.

"Mending a few broken doors isn't going to make anyone forget he killed people."

"He doesn't need anyone to forget," Maggie said stubbornly to the woman. Maybe it was too forward of her, but she said it anyway. "I think he just needs some forgiveness."

She was still working on forgiving him herself, but how could he ever manage that if she didn't give him a chance? After the conversations she'd had with him, she very much wanted to believe he would stick to his word and work off his severe debts with this town. That, and having the villagers still hate him and not trust in her would make things impossible. She loved Lightview. She wanted to help heal it, if she could.

Maggie still didn't trust him. And she knew she didn't have to, but it pained her to have all these malignant feelings towards him. The woman pursed her lips but said nothing else and turned to watch the mayor's house. She turned to Beatrice and gave a weak smile to her friend. "Thank you," she muttered.

"Are you going to be okay?" Bea squeezed Maggie's hand tightly. She still looked tired and weak to Beatrice. She might have healed physically, but whatever mental toll she was dealing with was a heavy one.

"Yes, thanks." A more genuine smile, then. "Go on and see your family. Tell them I said hello. I'll be around."

Beatrice was still unsure, but felt a little better at Maggie's reassuring expression. She hefted her bag more comfortably on her shoulder and nodded. "Okay. See you later, Magpie."

Maggie watched her go before turning to the pillar Basil had made the night of their battle. It loomed over the courtyard like a dark omen, but Maggie knew it wouldn't last. She placed a hand on it and heard herself sigh. The ground began to vibrate beneath her, and then the risen cobblestone, too. She looked back to see Basil drawing an invisible rune with his wand as he stepped towards her and the mess he had made during their battle.

Stepping back, the pillar seemed to slowly melt back into the ground and the cracked cobblestones around it mended. He had an arrogant look on his face, but when he looked at Magnolia and saw her expression, he became sullen again. "Sorry. Was I doing it again?"

"The look? Yes." She glanced around herself to see the villagers murmuring to each other, but they started to disperse and go on with their afternoon. Maggie felt relieved, but she knew they would be talking about this for days. Maybe that wasn't such a bad thing.

"Even if you can do something someone else can't," she told him, "you don't go around acting as though you're better than them. You're not. Everyone has worth." Being self-important and putting forth that hubris onto someone else only bred contempt, and Maggie didn't want anything to do with it. She wasn't afraid to tell him so.

Basil started to look taken aback and then stopped himself. It was clear he still didn't know her, but he did know she was right. Tom used to say, "No one is better than anyone." Basil always struggled with that. *But I know more, I can do more.* But he didn't know how to use tools, or how to use most electronics, or how to grow plants without magic... He rubbed the back of his neck uncomfortably, realizing his faults and, to distract himself from further shortcomings, pointed down the street with his other hand.

"I wrecked some roofs, we should probably head over and fix those, too."

Maggie nodded, a little relieved that he changed the topic on his own. "Go on ahead. I need to speak with the mayor."

The mayor was leaning on his cane and staring at his home when Maggie picked up her bag beside him. She fished a vial out and cleared her throat, as it seemed he hadn't noticed her yet.

"Oh, yes, Miss Magnolia." He twisted the end of his mustache as he looked down at her.

"Hello, Mayor. Did Basil do an alright job?"

"An excellent job, yes. He even went so far as to clean the chimney and magic the windows clean. My furniture and drapes are as good as new." He looked down at the vial in her hand and raised a brow in question.

Maggie looked to his gaze and handed the vial to him. "This'll calm your nerves, sir. I know it's been a hectic time...um. Are you sure you're happy with this arrangement?"

"Of course. I'd rather not make another grave. Would you?"

"No, of course not."

"Your uncle would be proud of that, I'm sure. Tom was a gem to this town. It's not always easy to learn the truth." The mayor heaved a heavy sigh and pushed his glasses up his nose once again. His hair looked all the grayer since the last time she saw him, as if it could get any more gray. "You're a strong young woman, Magnolia. I know you can handle this task." He winked at her and pocketed the vial she had handed him. "Thanks for the medicine. I'll be happy to take it. I hear you're a powerful potions master. If you ever need council, you know where to find me." He headed back inside his home, leaving Maggie alone in the courtyard. She headed back down the street to where Basil was and helped him mend the roofs.

CHAPTER ELEVEN

Cicadas sang their end of summer songs in the heat of the day, and still the sea breeze calmly swayed through the village, cooling Basil as his pale skin absorbed the season's sun on his bare back. Black pants didn't help the heat he felt but at least he had finally ditched the black tunic. He couldn't help it; black was a witch's color and he still liked to wear it proudly.

He was pulling back cobblestone and earth, like a wire cutting through wet clay, peeling it back so he could lay magic reinforced pipes and wiring. He was working on the other half of the electricity problem he'd started but never finished all those years ago.

Maggie didn't really understand what he was doing, or how he knew what he was doing. When he explained it to her, she tried to comprehend his method. But it just didn't stick, and Basil grew impatient with her quickly. So she left him to his devices and sat outside at a nearby cafe, sipping on some fresh lemonade, comfortable under the shade of her umbrella. Every so often she'd look up from her notebook that she had been scribbling potion ideas into, to check in on Basil's work.

Even though he was feeling a bit irritable, it was calming

work. He sometimes felt like he finally knew what Tom had been talking about during the time they had spent together: that hard work was good for the soul and all that. Sometimes he thought it was a crock of dung and quit angrily. But today, this had to get done, and he wanted to at least finish something he'd started.

There was a tap at his shoulder and Basil wiped his brow as he turned to see a man glaring at him. What insolence. His good mood would be shattered now.

"Why haven't you apologized to any of us personally?" the man demanded. A woman stood behind him; she must have been his wife. "Our children are dead because of you. You should be doing more than just fixing houses."

"They're dead," Basil snapped. "What do you expect me to do? I can't bring them back."

The wife came from behind her husband and punched Basil in the face. He expected a slap, but boy, was he wrong. He let out a quiet gasp of surprise, the attack momentarily blinding him in one eye. His hand instinctively went to where she hit him and he could feel his eye throbbing painfully. He felt his anger growing, slowly but surely, like a whale emerging from the depths.

"Don't bother me with this shit anymore," he retorted, the words biting but the anger deflating. "I'm sorry for what happened, but this is all I'm good for." He turned away from them to continue his work, biting his tongue all the while. The couple gave him an off-colored look before leaving him be, unable to get any more from him.

Maggie had jumped up from the table and ran half-way towards them. She expected Basil to lash out, but he simply turned away and the couple left him. Maggie tentatively stepped the rest of the way towards him, unsure as to how he would react. "Are you okay?" she asked.

Basil whipped around at her, lashing his arm out. It was full of magic, as wind swept up in its wake. Maggie froze, expecting to be pushed back, but it wasn't more than a fitful breeze.

His body was tense but Maggie found herself smiling a little. "I guess not," she answered herself, "but you're controlling yourself better."

The witch pushed his hair from his face and glanced at her, brow furrowed. "Sorry," he muttered. He went back to his work and Maggie stepped away, a little uncertain and with her hands clasped together behind her. She went back to her table and started to write out a letter to the couple. They didn't need to be bothered now; they looked to be grieving all over again. But maybe she could convince them to learn to accept the events as they were, and are.

She sighed. It was so much more difficult than that. Maybe she could convince Basil to be a little more...not so... difficult, or hard to be around.

She groaned and rubbed her face.

Basil tied his hair back in a low bun to get it away from his eyes before going back to fixing the roof on the Val's household and storefront. The damage ended up being a bit more extensive and his first fix had been an unfortunate failure. Thankfully, no one had been hurt, and this time, Basil had the courtesy to do the job right the second time instead of, well... Running away, as Magnolia would have so boldly reminded him. And for what it was worth, which was a lot for the black haired witch, the Vals were appreciative of his fix and improvements. He managed a real smile, and for much longer than usual, considering that he still got dirty looks from people from time to time.

Maggie had just stepped inside the general store with a fist full of popsicles for her friends when Old Nan brushed past her to step outside. It had been a week now since Maggie had woken and recovered and things were finally starting to get back to normal. She handed Bea and Canton their popsicles and thought nothing of the old woman stepping out for some air.

Standing in the street, both his arms in the air and sweat beading on his forehead, Basil was applying the final coat of magic for waterproofing the roof. He saw the old woman coming out from her shop from the corner of his eye and, despite his strain, tried to offer a friendly smile. It came off a little crooked, but it was a start.

An old, shriveled finger pointed right into his face. "You might be fixing things now," she said quietly, yet sternly, "but don't for a minute think I'll forgive you. You killed my husband and I hate you for it. The only reason I'm accepting your help is because I trust that Magnolia Hanna, and don't you forget it."

Basil had finished the coat and stared at the old woman as he lowered his arms. Besides Maggie, he had only been confronted by one other family he had inadvertently hurt because of his thoughtless mistakes. His first instinct was to tell her to sod off, like he had to the first family, that it was over now, but...he thought better on that. That would have just been yet another mistake. He was trying not to make those so easily anymore. He glanced at Maggie through the shop window and thought of her uncle.

The witch bowed his head deeply. "I don't deserve your forgiveness. There's nothing I can do to make it up to you, but I'll do everything I can to make things as comfortable for you all here as possible." He had learned why Magnolia had the respect she did, though it wasn't always easy to swallow. She was kind, and selfless. She thought of the consequences. Somehow she always managed to get through the adversity. He still didn't quite understand it, but he was trying to learn that, too.

Old Nan frowned all the more at Basil. "See that you do." And with that, she lifted her skirts and went back inside. Maggie came out shortly after, glancing back at Old Nan as she walked past. She looked at Basil suspiciously.

"Everything alright?"

Basil shrugged, as usual. "Maybe," he added. Maggie handed him the last popsicle. "Thank you." It was a hot day, one of the last days of summer, and he took to it immediately. Maggie was impressed. It didn't seem to pain him anymore to say his pleasantries, and whatever had happened between him and Old Nan hadn't ended in a screaming match. That was better than the fight she almost had to break up between him and another family. Thankfully he hadn't used any magic; he'd gotten a good black eye instead. Served him right, honestly, and at the time she wasn't afraid to tell him so.

The redhead smiled and shrugged in return. "No problem." It was easier to return said pleasantries now that he wasn't a whirling storm of grief and destruction. She still found a bit of worry creeping back into her mind about him every so often, though.

The shop's door jingled open and Canton poked his head through, looking over at Magnolia and Basil. "Hey, Magpie," he called. "Think you can pick up our lunch from the market? I'd do it myself, but we're a little busy..." He glanced back at the customers crowding around his sister and grandmother near a display case. He called to them to please be patient, and then returned a pleading gaze back to Maggie.

Maggie gave a sympathetic smile. "Sure."

"Great! Thanks so much. It's the Green Mer, just around the corner from the butcher. You remember?"

"Yeah, I know the place. I'll be back soon." Canton went back inside, so Maggie turned her attention to Basil. "You still have work to do here?"

"Yes. Just a few things, some touch ups. The roof's done, anyway."

"Okay. See you in a few, then." She mounted her broom and the wind gently caressed her into the air. Casually, she sailed down the street, just high enough to not bother any pedestrians walking around. She was pleased to find that the looks she got now weren't of anger or suspicion, but of joy and curiosity. She felt more free than she had in a while, and in a way...it was thanks to Basil. But only because he had been awful, and she wasn't going to thank him for that.

It was busy at the market, but it was lunch time so that was a given. When she landed in the square, people were crowding around her and she wondered if it might be even busier than usual. What she wasn't expecting was that they were all crowding for *her*. She looked around quickly, a little haggard at being jostled as they came up to her, thanking her.

"Oh, Maggie, thank you so much."

"Magnolia, you've been a dream!"

"Mags! Thank you for saving our town!"

Maggie blushed, flustered, and held her broom tight to herself as she looked around the crowding faces. She was being thanked for her potions, for helping the town, for taking care of Basil... She felt overwhelmed, but she smiled anyway, and nodded and said her pleasantries.

"You're welcome, it was my pleasure, of course."

Someone small held her from behind and she turned to see a little girl hugging her waist. She laughed and patted the girl's head as she said to Maggie, "Thank you!" in a small voice. It seemed as though everyone in Lightview was buzzing about the improvements and change of heart they were experiencing, at least, towards Maggie. They were still wary of the dark clothed witch, and were wont to express it despite the time it had been since the incident.

Maggie slipped out from the crowd in the courtyard to the open hall along the indoor businesses. The villagers had gotten distracted with their retelling of Magnolia's battle with Basil and she found herself chuckling a little as someone expressed a large exaggeration over her "control" of Basil.

Basil Olivander would not have enjoyed such an exaggeration. Well, she decided, he'd get over it. Maybe he'd even laugh about it.

The Green Mer was a cafe and restaurant. They focused on

local fare, usually for lunch or dinner, but also served coffee and pastries for the morning and brunch crowd. It actually did quite well, as Maggie could tell when she stepped inside and saw most of the booths and tables filled. It looked like a mermaid had taken root in the cafe, with faux seaweed and floating glass globes hanging with macrame from the ceilings and against the walls. It was charming and interesting, and probably one of the more creative businesses in the town.

At the counter, Maggie gave Canton's name and was given a large, reinforced paper bag of food. The Vals had a tab here, so she put the food in a fabric bag she had tied to her broom and headed back to the general store, getting up in the air on her broom before she got stuck again in the crowds.

Back at the Val's, Basil was collecting materials and cleaning up. Canton looked up from the counter when Maggie entered the store and grinned. "Great, I'm starved. There's food in there for you and Basil, too."

Surprised, Maggie handed off the bag and collected Basil from the front. They met everyone in the back kitchen, where there was a table for them all to sit. Old Nan and Mr. and Mrs. Val took theirs upstairs, but the four unlikely others sat at the table, almost like a family. Basil was trying not to feel like the hellish babysitter, and Maggie thought that maybe he was more like the odd uncle, twice removed, perhaps.

The lunch consisted of a salad, fish, and buttered bread. There were nuts and small fruit in the salad, too, and it all smelled delicious. It made Maggie's mouth water; she hadn't realized how hungry she was. There was a small container of lemon juice that she grabbed and poured some over her fish before digging in. "Thanks for the meal."

She knocked her foot into Basil's at his silence and he lifted his head from his food. "Thank you."

The three friends' conversation was animated and lively. They laughed and talked about their day, and all the while Basil sat, eating quietly and listening. Since he had been living with Magnolia, though sometimes sleeping in his tent outside, he had been forced to spend time with the three of them. It had been a bit aggravating at first, but as he was easing into this new lifestyle, he was noticing more about people's behavior. It was, actually, kind of nice. He found that he was smiling.

It was hard to listen to people, for Basil. They didn't know much, or anything, about magic. Their reactions were usually hostile or unsure, and their lack of faith in his ability just made him angry. He knew more than them. He knew *better*. That is, until he had mucked it all up and started to doubt himself, too. He had thought he was so superior, and that magic was the most superior way to do, well, anything. Other ways were primitive, arbitrary. The only person he had ever trusted without magic was Tom.

Basil sighed. It was a quiet sigh, and no one else seemed to notice it.

Others weren't so forgiving of his mistakes. He wondered if he'd ever forgive himself, too. For a while he thought there had been no need for forgiveness; he had believed it was someone else's fault. Not his problem.

Of course, that was denial and misplaced responsibility. He had been a fool.

Maggie had been patient. But she had been firm with her independence and idea of respect. He had slipped a few times, insulting her as he taught her something magic related and she hadn't gotten it right away. For once, he had felt bad about his own behavior. He apologized. He was doing a lot of that these days.

It was humbling, to say the least.

Maggie's hand was on his shoulder and he looked up from his empty plate to her, who was smiling gently at him. "Ready to go home?" It had been a long day and she could tell Basil was tired. He had been working hard since early that morning.

Sometimes he forgot how old he was, and how young she was. He could have been her father, well, maybe he was exaggerating—but here she was taking care of him. He ran a hand through his hair, faintly smiled, and nodded. "Yes. Let's go."

CHAPTER TWELVE

It was a beautiful evening, perfect for the Harvest Festival. The sky was clear of clouds, showing deep blues across the horizon, and the stars sat bright against the backdrop, unimpeded by the waning moon. They might not have had the full harvest moon, but it was fall now and everyone was just happy to be celebrating. Despite the new season, it still felt warm out, but the sea breeze kept them cool and comfortable as usual.

Every building Maggie saw was covered in strings of lights, some white, some colorful, and there were small flags hanging, too, shining through from the lights. Music could be heard in the direction of the courtyard and marketplace, but on the streets it was mostly the chatter of pedestrians and laughter of children heading to the main event.

Maggie wore high-waisted dark brown pants with silver buttons lining up the sides, and a cream colored tunic halfway tucked in with sleeves that went to her elbows. Her hair was down but each side had some pulled back to keep her hair from her face. Her witch's hat sat proudly upon her head, and she wore it with little black boots. Beatrice had put a string of lavender in her hair, too, for good measure. She had her bag around her shoulder, and as was all too normal now, it was full of potions. But these ones were a bit different.

Basil wasn't far behind. Maggie was giving him free reign to do as he pleased during the festival, but he found himself following her to the square anyway. He hadn't admitted it, but he was interested in what happened at a festival. He had never been to one. When he had lived in Lightview before, he had avoided the festival like the plague. All those people, all those questions, and all of that...mess. He was wearing his typical black garb, but Beatrice had put some lavender in his hair, too. She had told him it looked cute and he hadn't really had the heart to tell her no. That was a big surprise for all of them.

Honestly, Basil had been doing a good job. He deserved to have some time on his own, and Maggie wasn't the only one who thought so. It wasn't just the work he was doing, it was in his attitude. She felt like, maybe, he was finally enjoying himself.

Maggie, Canton, and Bea were all walking together and entered the marketplace where all of the delicious fragrances were coming from. Food was being cooked in the open booths and there were more people there than Maggie had ever seen. It wasn't just people from Lightview, but Westdown and even the next town over, too.

The shops and booths, much like the homes and other buildings, were also decorated with lights and flags and other colorful baubles. There were lights shaped like fish that hung welcome signs from their mouths at the seafood booths, and stars that looked convincingly like starfish.

The trio stopped at one booth to get snacks on a stick. Maggie got one of fruit, Canton had one of vegetables, and Bea got one of fried octopus. She said it was chewy, but savory, and made it a point to mention she wanted to try all things seafood. She claimed it was for research. Further down towards the courtyard they found a game booth where you tossed rings onto bottles to earn a prize.

"I got it!" Canton cheered and he walked away with a

stuffed animal cat, which he gave to his pouting sister that hadn't gotten a single ring. It was a surprise to each of them, normally their situation was reversed, and they laughed together about it.

Maggie spied Mikel and Prairie with the Williams family at a larger booth selling cider and fruit wine.

"You made it!" Mikel boomed as he lifted a glass of wine into the air. He stepped out from behind the booth and gave Magnolia a tight hug with one large arm. "This is the wine you made, Magpie. It's delicious!"

"And it's selling great," old Mr. Williams said as he sold another two cups. He poured three more and offered them to the trio.

"That's wonderful." Canton grinned.

"Thank you! I'm glad we were helpful." Maggie took one and drank it slowly. She could hardly taste the fermentation at all, it was so sweet and flavorful.

"How are you enjoying the festival?" Mikel asked. "I told you it'd be a doozy. The kids loved the maze during the day, too."

Maggie grinned. "It's really fun and everyone is so happy. I can't believe how many people are here." They had gotten to do the maze earlier that day as well, but it was too dark to enjoy it now. "I hear it's a big hit every time. The boats all looked so nice, too!" The ships had paraded down the coast, all decorated with lights just as the sun had set. With Lightview being the only place she had ever experienced such a large body of water, the boats had been especially exciting to see dressed up.

"It gets bigger every year," Prairie said from behind the table. "But it's how we make that extra penny and it's great for the harvest." She had her arm around her son, who was all red in the face from his wine. He grinned at them and raised his glass as if in salute.

Maggie chuckled at that and waved them all goodbye as they continued on through the town. There were game booths with slingshots, popping balloons, paper boats and mechanical horses. There were more sweet shops than she could count, each of them appealing in their own way. The colors were dazzling and bright and fun. It was like a dream! The music finally reached its peak when the trio made it to the courtyard. A band played in the center, a fun and loud foot-stomping tune that made Maggie want to dance. She noticed Basil on the other end of the courtyard, leaning against the leg of a gate and tapping his fingers against his crossed arms. She grinned all the more, and it seemed infectious because everyone in the town happened to be grinning or smiling, too.

The witch felt it was finally time. She slipped away from Bea and Canton as they danced together in the courtyard and sat her bag down in the grass. Her potions clinked together quietly, almost silent in the fight to be heard against the band, and she pulled one out. It glowed purple and fuchsia and swirled around the glass as if it was alive. She uncorked it and poured it into the street.

The liquid fell out of the bottle like a mist, slow and moving of its own accord. It spread out, much larger than the space of the bottle, and coalesced into the shape of a deer. It looked back at Maggie with blank eyes, its antlers tall and glowing, and then darted off into the crowd, a trail of mist dissipating behind it. She heard gasps, and then laughter and awe, and so she took another bottle out. This one was teal, made of the same stuff as the deer mist, but when she poured it out, it didn't spread as much. It formed into a rabbit and hopped away into a crowd of children.

Maggie unloaded the rest of her bottles. There was a green fox, a flying yellow fish, a red otter, an orange cat, a blue wolf, and finally, a small, but bigger than the other animals, white dragon. This one had been tricky, as dragons hadn't existed in, well, who could remember? Maybe never. But it looked pretty spot on from the picture books Maggie had read when she was a child, and it got the biggest reaction.

The mist animals were interacting with the crowd, the fox rubbing its misty body against and through children's legs, the cat jumping on a booth's table and acting as though it would take the food, but just phasing through it as its paw attempted the grab. The creatures could float and behaved much like a ghost would, except they were far from frightening.

"This is what you were working on?" Maggie jumped, having been snuck up on as she had packed away the empty bottles. It was only Basil.

"You scared me!" She laughed, standing up. She slung her bag over her shoulder. "Why, you don't like it?" She stuck her tongue out playfully.

"They're done very well," Basil said quietly. "Everyone seems to love them."

"Maybe you can make something even better next year?" she suggested, smiling.

Basil didn't reply, but he did smile.

There was an explosion overhead and Maggie looked up in awe as the fireworks started. Bea and Canton ran up to them and each held one of her hands, laughter in their eyes.

"They're shooting from the barge in the bay," Canton said, the colors reflecting off his glasses.

"I've never seen anything like it." Maggie gasped as a flower bloomed in the sky. She squeezed her friends' hands and then released them to step further into the courtyard, closer to the band. "Let's dance more!" And so she did, and her friends followed suit, dancing in the crowd as the fireworks boomed overhead, and the colorful animals misted through the villagers and between them as if they were trees in the forest.

Basil laughed. Actually laughed, and wiped at one eye with the knuckle of a finger. Tom would have liked this. He would have been dancing, too. But Basil had to push those thoughts aside. He had grieved enough, for now. Presently, he wanted to enjoy the fruits of his labor, and the labor of everyone here. It was amazing that so much had been done, both without his help and without magic. He wasn't the center of the universe, and if he hadn't started to change his attitude, no one would have even cared he was there. But he was noticing more friendly glances. He had even received a few thank yous, and good jobs. He used to ignore praise, especially when it came from someone who didn't practice magic.

"I'm impressed." An old man twisted his mustache with one hand and tapped his cane on the cobblestone with the other.

Basil, slightly surprised, saw that it was the mayor that had snuck up on him, much like Basil had done to Maggie. He shrugged then and looked back out into the crowd. "Me too."

"Are you glad to be alive?" He gave the witch a mysterious look and Basil found himself averting his gaze from the old man, unsure as to why it made him uncomfortable. Maybe because Basil was essentially asking for death not even a month ago. Because Maggie, or the mayor himself, could have killed him with just a word.

"Yes." It was a short and simple reply. He didn't feel he needed to give an explanation.

"Magnolia Hanna is a good girl." The mayor cleared his throat. "A young woman," he corrected himself. "Don't let her down." He tipped his hat and strolled off into the crowd.

Cryptic as usual, it seemed. But, it did the trick. Basil felt more determined than ever, and whatever self-deprecating thoughts that had been swirling in his head were quelled by his will. He left the courtyard to go back to the market and bought himself something to eat, whistling while he did. The orange cat-mist trailed behind him and phased between and through his legs.

It was late now and the fireworks show had finished. The band was playing more quietly, and people were starting to go back to their homes, or to the inn. Mikel's booth had sold out of both food and drink and they were already packed up by the time the trio passed their booth again.

"Oh, we could have helped," Beatrice said, sounding almost disappointed.

Mikel laughed. "Yer job was to have fun. Did you?"

"It was amazing!" Maggie raised her arms above her head in excitement, fists clenched and then opened to emphasize said enthusiasm.

"Did you see the dragon?" Canton asked him, grinning like he knew a secret.

"Sure did. That was a mighty fine bit of magic you did there, girly." He guffawed and patted her on the shoulder. "I ain't seen a dragon since a lad in them story books. Brought me back."

Maggie grinned, and she walked Bea and Canton back to their home. They hugged goodbye and laughed over some of the events of the night before disappearing inside. Maggie looked around for Basil on the street, but she hadn't seen him. She figured he was back home already. She pulled out her broom and flew back to the lighthouse, its light shining ever onward for the ships at sea, and now, she supposed, for a witch.

The wind rippled the grass and wildflowers like seaweed on the ocean floor, alive with water and life, dancing. The tree beside the house was growing back nicely, new branches already sprouted and growing new leaves. A white flower bloomed where Maggie had never seen one grow before. She didn't realize the tree had flowers at all.

"It's a magnolia." Basil sat on the porch. He hadn't let himself in and was simply waiting for her return.

"Me?" She pointed at herself, and then looked back up at the tree. She laughed, suddenly. "I've never seen one before. It's beautiful."

Basil shrugged, like he always did. But he was smiling.

"You could have gone inside," she offered.

"It's too nice a night. I didn't wait long."

Maggie made her way up the path to the steps, her broom

in hand. "Looks like you enjoyed yourself."

"I did, actually," he finally admitted. Maggie smiled.

"I think it's time you went to visit my uncle's grave," Maggie said, suddenly serious. Her smile was still there, but it was a little sad.

"Is it that time already?" Basil asked quietly. He didn't know if he would have ever gotten the chance to see it. He was still smiling, too, but the tears had come. If it was grief, or happiness, or both, he didn't know.

"Oh, don't cry." Maggie put her hand on his shoulder. She was tearing up, too.

"Thank you." It was the most sincere thanks he'd given yet. Maybe he didn't deserve the kindness, but he would accept it. And one day it would be enough. For Tom, for Maggie. For himself.

Things had turned out alright for Magnolia Hanna. The town was happy again and more accepting of magic. She thought she'd done a pretty decent job and she was proud of herself. Dealing with Basil, well... That had been entirely unexpected, and difficult. She didn't think she would have made it through. This was only the beginning, neither of them were done yet, but in the short time she had known him she could tell that something in him had changed. She felt they could learn a lot from each other, and maybe a visit to her family would be good for the both of them. Plus...they both needed a bit more closure.

So for now, there would be one more witch in the lighthouse.

ABOUT THE AUTHOR

Azalea Forrest is a fantasy author living with her partner, two cats, and leopard gecko in sunny Florida. Her stories focus on hope and adventure, being a better person, coping with mental illness, and doing your best. She loves getting inside a character's head to learn who they are.

Aside from writing, she is also a photographer, editor, and gamer. Described as a "living Ghibli character", Forrest wants to spread a little more light in the world. She is affiliated with Mathematician Records, where you can buy her books directly. You can find her on Twitter at @aforrestwrites, Facebook at @azaleaforrest, and Instagram at @aforrestwrites, as well as her websites listed below.

azaleaforrest.wordpress.com
mathematicianrecords.com/book

Please consider leaving a review: ratings will help other readers find this book.
All review links can be found at Forrest's Bio Link in this QR code.
bio.link/azaleaforrest

ALSO BY AZALEA FORREST

The Underground	A Bitter Drink

No sparkles or romance here. Join the vampire Ashai through city streets as she hunts for her bar's arsonist alongside werewolves and ghosts. Full of supernaturals, Ash winds up in The Underground, a lawless place, at the edge of a war that could end their masquerade forever.

Full of misadventure, A Bitter Drink tangles Rowan in the vines after catching a peer talking treason. He's forced to team up with a vagabond, an elven spy, and a calming dwarf, but his heart isn't in it. The plantman's a coward and he knows it. To change would be a bitter drink indeed.

Made in United States
Orlando, FL
30 November 2022

25273807R00081